ABOUT THE AUTHOR

MR. JOHN ROEBURT—ex-newspaperman, novelist, screen, television and radio writer.

A Winner of the "Edgar," an award presented to him by the Mystery Writers of America for his *Inner Sanctum* thrillers.

A native of New York City, he covered the night police courts in his early days, affording him a first-hand view of the city's "denizens of the night." Going through the depression years, he took a clerical job in a bank. But jotting down figures only intensified his desire to write. Next, he landed in Hollywood, where, after several years of misadventures, he returned, married, raised a family and ran a couple of antique shops. His head filled with plots, he padlocked his stores and bought a typewriter.

Today, Mr. Roeburt is one of this country's finest mystery writers. We think that in *Tough Cop*, Mr. Roeburt is at his top-best.

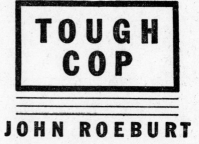

TOUGH COP

JOHN ROEBURT

GRAPHIC PUBLICATIONS

First Graphic Printing, May, 1950
Second Graphic Printing, September, 1951
Third Graphic Printing, April, 1953
Fourth Graphic Printing, January, 1956

Complete and Unabridged

Graphic Publishing Company, Inc.
240 West 40 Street
New York, N. Y.

PRINTED IN THE UNITED STATES OF AMERICA

CHAPTER ONE

1.

The muscular fellow in the barber chair drew one foot in, then set the other on the shoe-shine box. The shine boy dabbed cream on the toe, then flipped the rag vigorously across the shoe. The closing strains of the *Star-Spangled Banner* emptied into the room, and New York City's own station went off the air. The shine boy went to the wall radio.

"Off," the man in the chair ordered. "I can't hear myself think."

The barber set his scissors down, and selected a bottle from a shelf.

The patron shook his head. "No tonic, Tony. Just comb it dry."

Tony worked the comb, pushed an unruly forelock back on the head, completed a few final pats, then held a square mirror to the rear of the patron's head.

Tony said affectionately, "Like a movie actor, Mr. Devereaux."

Devereaux grimaced into the large wall mirror. Opaque cheeks and a thin, aquiline nose with a broken bridge grimaced back at him. "Movie actor named Boris Karloff," he said wryly.

Devereaux got off the chair nimbly, recovered his coat from a wall peg, got into it, and then, before departing, gave the room with the single barber chair a last lingering look.

There were streamers in red, white, and blue strung from the ceiling lights, a mammoth cutout of a face that looked like Mr. Devereaux, and was, and the wall mirrors were soaped with print that said repetitiously, "Good Luck, Johnny Devereaux."

More than an intimate barbershop, this back room in a celebrated night club was a mirror of the importance of its patrons. Not moneyed importance, but achievement and color, the special and extraordinary color of glamorous people who were actors, columnists, round-the-world fliers, zanies; the famous and the infamous—and topflight detectives. Johnny Devereaux was, or had been, a topflight detective.

"Reads like an epitaph." Devereaux smiled regretfully. "Hey, I'm not dead. Just retired."

Tony's face creased seriously. "Excuse me, Mr. Devereaux. But why you retire?" His eyes shone admiration. "So young. Like a boy yet."

"A gray-bearded boy," Devereaux said. "I'm tired of knocking heads together, Tony. Tired of being a tough cop in a world of shills, con men, killers, and plain crooks." His face clouded slightly. "I used to read good books, improve my mind, a long time ago, Tony. I want to pick up where I left off twenty years ago. I want to pick myself up and start traveling before I run out of time. Understand?"

Tony nodded doubtfully, opened a drawer, then came over with a book and a fountain pen. He uncorked the pen. "You autograph the book, Mr. Devereaux?" he said.

The dust jacket showed a newsreel montage of Manhattan scenes, and the type across it read: *Twenty Years a Cop*, by Johnny Devereaux.

Devereaux scribbled inside the cover, restored the pen and the book to the barber, then placed a ten-dollar bill on the wall ledge. "Buy a drink on me," he said fondly. At the door, he gestured at the soaped mirrors. "And hire yourselves a window washer."

The shine boy's face shone, and the barber blew a kiss.

2

Outside the club, with handshakes and good wishes finally in limbo, Devereaux slid behind the wheel of his brand-new Buick convertible—a farewell gift from the Department.

He sat stock-still, then began jingling his key ring moodily. What, he wondered, already feeling the burden of sudden freedom after decades in harness, did a man in retirement do with his time? He fingered the ignition key. Where, he ruminated sadly, now feeling a little old and used up, did retired detectives pasture?

He looked into the street and read the signs as far as his eye could reach:

IN PERSON—BILLIE HOLIDAY,
THE THREE LESTERS,
SUGAR JOHNSON—BOOGIE-WOOGIE PIANIST.

The row of after-theater clubs was just off Broadway. It was past midnight on a routine Tuesday night. The pushing throngs had disintegrated, and the few stragglers reeling under the shock of alcohol dragged into his focus in tortured slow motion. Taxicabs were glued bumper to bumper, their motors asleep and their drivers drowsing.

Devereaux sighed, and turned the key in the ignition.

The motor had coughed, awakening, when he saw her duck around the doorman and run to his car. She slammed the door

"Hurry, please!" Her voice behind him was urgent.

"Ditching someone?"

"Yes."

"Why my car?"

"Hurry, please!" She was close to tears.

Devereaux swung out from the curb in quick, automatic movements, oddly happy for the activity, grateful for the distraction. The Buick reached the avenue and turned into it.

"Who were you ditching?" he asked after a while

"My father."

"Under age?"

"I'm twenty."

"Past the age of consent." He signaled a car ahead, then passed it. "So what's the problem?"

"He's—unreasonably possessive."

A red light showed and Devereaux stopped, then turned to survey her. Baby-faced, red-headed, cream-cheeked—a treat to the eye. Unspoiled looking; a budding flower in a cellophane wrapper.

"Why take you clubbing, then? Drunks are bound to make passes"

"He didn't. Take me clubbing, I mean. He followed us."

The light showed green and the Buick loafed along at twenty-five. "Sneak off to City Hall with the boy friend," Devereaux said. "That will kill Pop's penchant for following you."

"It's not so simple as that." He felt her sigh. "Even if I were in love, I'd be afraid to—to marry."

Her tone revealed more than what was said. Fear, he adduced it to be. The pent-up fear of someone too taut to cry out. It engaged Devereaux, piqued his imagination. He swung out of avenue traffic and nestled into the curb.

"You're out of danger now." Devereaux smiled. "Maybe you'd like to come up front and just sit a while?"

She came to sit beside him, and he stared at her curiously. The make-up, if she wore any, was subtle; the hair-do enhanced the very young impression she gave. There was nothing in her face that he could read, nothing of the tensions he sensed in her. The fear he had detected was only evident in the small fluttering of her hands.

"You're really in trouble, huh?" he said.

She nodded, and as her head came forward slightly, he looked into her eyes. The tensions that weren't evident in her face lived in her eyes. He smiled at her sympathetically, and watched her draw her underlip in. Tears were close; a kind word would precipitate a flood.

He said gently, "Suppose I keep eyes strictly front while you let go and cry yourself out?" He saw the tears start down her cheeks, and turned severely front. Not long after, when the noises of grief had died away, he turned to face her.

Devereaux said, "In my time, lots of people have used me as a father-confessor. All kinds of people."

She smiled gratefully at him with moist eyes, and his pulse quickened. He stared at her, surprised at her effect on him. Beautiful, he thought to himself regretfully. This unspoiled girl dabbing at her eyes was not the fruit of his forties.

"How bad is it?" he prompted.

"It's a mess," she said, accepting him as a confidant.

"Father a completely bad actor?"

"Yes."

"A tyrant, eh?"

"Much worse than a tyrant." She hesitated, and there was a look of revulsion in her eyes that haunted his imagination. He picked at the bits she had told him, and brought them closer to his thinking. Reviewing them, they seemed little against the violent emotional currents in the girl. Domineering fathers, like possessive mothers, were a commonplace. The iron fist and the silver cord—as a policeman he'd encountered both more often than not.

He looked at her doubtfully, at a loss, and then his imagination leaped. Much worse than a tyrant, she had said, with revulsion showing in her eyes. He looked at her searchingly, watched shame flushing her cheeks.

"What do you do, if anything?" he said after a long, awkward moment.

"I dance."

"Ballet?"

She nodded. "Modern. The Graham School."

"Professionally?"

"I hope to, ultimately."

"Live home?" Devereaux smiled. "Shut me up any time you like."

"I live home."

"Why not make a break, keep house on your own?"

She drew a long breath. "I can't."

"You mean," Devereaux pressed, "your father won't allow it?"

"Yes. My father won't allow it," she said, and her tone told him clearly of bonds and bondage. He waited through a short silence, hoping her bursting need to talk would prevail. He was right. She said, "If he is my father."

"Don't you know?" Devereaux exclaimed.

"No. I mean, I don't know"—she fumbled for words—"I don't know for certain that he is."

"But what makes you think that he's not?"

"It's something vague." A hand moved nervously to her face. "It's what he is, the feeling I have about him. I don't feel him to be my father."

Devereaux said impatiently, "Is there something *actual* that makes you doubt this man is your father?"

"Just impressions." Her hand moved as if brushing something impeding her vision. "Impressions only."

Devereaux regarded her critically. There were strong suggestions of irrationality, even hoax, but the emotional distress was real, and the girl had breeding and intelligence. Intelligence, unmistakably. It was in her face and speech and manner.

"I take it, then," Devereaux said, accepting her as rational and believable, "that there is no infancy-to-now association with him in your recollection. This man, your father, is something recent in your experience?"

"Yes." She smiled weakly. "Or is it no? He is recent—comparatively, that is. And I have no real infancy recollection of him."

"When did you first become aware of him as your father?"

"When I was ten. From then on, all through my school life, there were visits, gifts, vacations away with him. But always estranged, never close. In a family sense, I mean. Then, last year, he brought me home to live with him."

"You boarded out through your school years?"

"Yes. Through school and finishing school."

"And absolutely no recollections of him prior to your tenth birthday?"

"No. Earlier, I merely knew *of* him, but vaguely."

"How did you know *of* him?"

"From teachers in school, I suppose. From an occasional letter read to me."

"Didn't you wonder about it? Kids, even in tender years, have a strong interest in where they came from, a great curiosity about whom they belong to."

She shook her head. "I didn't wonder about it. Not consciously, anyhow." Her face clouded. "Not having a home, in the true sense, I found my adjustment in the school, in my teachers. I remember believing that all children belonged to their schoolmistress and teachers, and to the school itself. I think I believed it quite normal to have a father in some shadowy somewhere who wrote letters and sent occasional gifts."

"And when you were ten, he came out of his, ah, shadowy somewhere, emerged as an identity, a person?"

"Yes. He appeared suddenly, just before my tenth birthday."

"Did you accept him as your father then?"

"Yes."

"Affectionately, glad for a parent?"

13

She was remembering. "No. At first I resented him, I think. Later, I became afraid of him."

"Why?"

"He had a way of staring at me, a frightening way of looking at me coldly and critically, as if I were a purchase he had to make up his mind about."

"He gave you this feeling every time you met?"

"Until my fourteenth birthday. After that, he changed. I could feel the change."

Devereaux prompted gently, "As if he'd decided to make the purchase?"

She smiled at him gratefully and nodded her head. "His attitude became fanatically possessive. He transferred me to another school, a more expensive one, and began to shower me with fine clothes, costly presents."

"And these attentions didn't bring you closer to him?"

"No. If anything, I resented him more, became more afraid. The clothes were far too grown-up, too sophisticated, for my age. I was fourteen, and there were negligées, gowns made by Parisian *couturières*. I felt indecent in them, and finally burned them in the school incinerator when my teachers began to look strangely at me, when my classmates began to whisper about me." She shuddered, and her voice seemed to shrink. "There were imported perfumes when I was fifteen. And with every birthday there were hideously gaudy shoes with higher heels than before. I remember monstrous six-inch spikes that came on my sixteenth birthday."

Devereaux interrupted the disturbing memories. "And these things made you suspect that he wasn't really your father?"

"Does it sound like what a father would do?"

"Not the—er—usual father. What about your mother? Know anything about her?"

She shook her head. "He says she ran off when I was a baby, and was never heard from since. Before my tenth birthday, I had some attachment for a woman who ran a private home for waifs. I lived with her for a while, some-where in the outskirts of a city, before I was placed in boarding school."

"Remember her name?"

"I remember her as a Mrs. Jennings," she said doubtfully.

"Can't remember the whereabouts of that private home, I suppose?"

"No. But I've seen Mrs. Jennings. Anyhow, I think it was Mrs. Jennings."

"Where?"

"Visiting my father. About a week ago."

"Did you speak to her?"

"No. My father prevented that. He shouldered me out of the library quite obviously. I'd come upon them unexpect-edly."

Devereaux sighed involuntarily. It was his first feeling of solid ground. "Get any impressions from what you saw of them together?" he asked.

"Yes. There was hostility between them. I heard nothing said, but Father seemed barely able to control his rage."

Devereaux said reflectively, "I don't suppose you'd know where to locate this Mrs. Jennings—if she *is* your Mrs. Jen-nings?"

"I do," she said, and Devereaux looked his surprise. "She's registered at the Hotel Orleans as Mrs. Minna Gordon."

"How do you know?"

"I followed her home that night."

"Why haven't you visited her, spoken to her?"

"I lack the courage."

"But to inquire into your background, prove or dissolve your doubts?"

"I'm afraid. And I'm alone." Her voice dropped to a barely audible key. "I'm just frightened all the time—as though something terrible was going to happen. To me."

A silence fell. Devereaux reached into a dashboard com-partment, found his cigarette pack, extracted one, gestured the pack at the girl, and then, surprised at her eager nod, held it closer to her. He worked an enameled lighter and held the flare out to her, letting the illumination linger for an instant.

She was more composed now; talk and tears had been a catharsis. Her eyes were bright, their depths unrevealed. They seemed remarkably free of their earlier pain; seemed curiously flat as they fixed upon his face expectantly, as if their burden had passed to him in some mystical transference.

Devereaux withdrew the flare and brought it to his own cigarette. He drew in smoke and exhaled it, thinking. Should he really involve himself? Sucker, he thought irritably, as the awareness grew that the decision had already been made for him. His first busybody peek inside her had borne an implicit offer of help. That was how it was with him. Would he, he wondered, eyeing her in a lingering side-long look, ally himself with her need if she were fat and fifty?

"No birth certificate?" he asked suddenly, taking charge of her problem.

"No. It was destroyed in a fire. This was in St. Paul. I've only school certificates as proof of birth." Her tone now took his stewardship almost for granted.

"How do you know a fire destroyed your birth record?"

"He told me so."

"Did you check?"

"Yes. I wrote the Town Clerk. He wrote back that the Hall of Records had burned to the ground fifteen years ago."

After a moment, Devereaux said, "I suppose it's idiotic of me to ask whether you bear the same name as this man—your father."

"We bear the same name, of course."

Devereaux puffed rapidly, then flipped the cigarette into the street. "I might be able to help," he began slowly, facing her. "Maybe let you lean a little." His eyes pinched at the corners in a shrewd, searching look. "*If* you were completely honest."

There was a betraying start, then a look of bewilderment that was palpably forced came into her face. Devereaux said forbiddingly, "Lie, and I'll dump you into the street on your lovely, lovely bottom." His tone softened. "Now, how did you happen into the back of my car?"

"Why, I—I left the Club Fifty-Two so hurriedly, in panic." She stopped, staring at his warning look. "You don't believe me, do you?"

"No, I don't. Furthermore, I don't believe anyone was after you, *or* that you were running from anyone, *or* that you were out with a boy friend, *or* that you were even at the Club Fifty-Two. And I *do* believe you landed in my car according to plan, by design, and by choice."

He saw the awe filling her face, and for the life of him he couldn't help chuckling. "Nothing really uncanny, nor is it any extrasensory perception, believe me. It's a simple matter of propriety and twenty yards. Propriety wouldn't permit an obviously proper young lady to enter a stranger's automobile, whatever her haste and panic. And there was a taxicab parked twenty yards closer to the door of Club Fifty-Two than my car. Any fugitive, especially a frightened young lady handicapped by high heels, would run into the nearest available taxicab." He looked at her for confirmation, watched her nod miserably, then resumed. "Those twenty yards and ordinary propriety, plus your great readiness to confide in me, make me certain that you picked my car, picked me, deliberately."

"You're right, in everything you've said," she finally conceded in wilted tones. "I did pretend to run out of Club Fifty-Two, and I did pick you deliberately." She seemed to droop. "I suppose you disbelieve everything I've told you now."

"Shouldn't I?"

"It's all true," she said hollowly.

"All right, then. I believe you."

"Will you help me?" Her fingers were touching him.

"Yes," he promised in a rush, then stopped, again surprised at her effect on him. His pulse was quickening, and there was a warmth flowing through him that he fought against showing in his face. Cavalier, and nothing more, he told himself sternly. He drew his arm away from her fingers. "Just how did you come to pick me as your champion?"

"I'd heard about you, read about you in the papers all week long." Her voice bubbled with admiration. "Fascinating stories about your twenty years as a detective. About how wise you are, and how clever."

It was flattery and he'd had much of it—up to his neck—but coming from her it was excitingly new. "Spare my blushes," he said.

"I tried to see you yesterday, right after that farewell banquet they gave you. But there were too many people around you then."

"Tell me your name," Devereaux said.

"Jennifer Phillips."

"And Mr. Whosis—which Phillips is he?"

There was a small hesitation. "Martin Phillips."

Devereaux's jaw fell. "Don't tell me!" he said incredulously.

"Yes," she nodded solemnly. "*The* Martin Phillips."

Devereaux whistled. Martin Phillips, the grand slam among theater critics. The high priest of literature who used rattlesnake venom for ink. The man who said that the drama had died with Shakespeare, that glamour was buried with Queen Victoria.

"He's a damned important figure, your so-called father," Devereaux said soberly.

"I know," she agreed dismally. Her fingers found his arm again. "Will you help me?"

"What was the name of that hotel?"

"The Orleans."

"What does this Mrs. Jennings, or Mrs. Gordon look like?"

"Gray-haired. About sixty, I'd say. Pale, like a sick person. Small, almost daintily small." Her eyes shone at him and her voice was fervent. "Thank you so very much."

"You're a little premature," Devereaux said. "Now, where can I drop you?"

CHAPTER TWO

1.

THE ORLEANS: A FAMILY HOTEL was a throwback to the era of horse cars and nickel beer. An incongruous neon sign across its face was the only concession to twentieth-century vogues. The Buick slid into the curb, parallel with a sidewalk stanchion that warned: *"No Parking, 8 a.m. to 6 p.m.*

It was forenoon. The outdoors was as sultry as an unseasonable September could be, and the street was a bedlam of people and motor traffic. Devereaux had got to the sidewalk when the whistle arrested him and a cop on horseback came galloping up.

"Don't you read, or should the sign say positively?" the cop on horseback said witheringly.

"Hiya, Kennedy." Devereaux submitted his face smilingly.

"Devereaux!" The voice chided. "Thought you were catching a train or a boat."

"Tomorrow. One fine tomorrow." Devereaux shrugged. "New York won't let go, Kennedy."

The street filled with a mad warfare of horns, and Kennedy, motioning Devereaux to wait, shooed a backing truck away from an area whose curb sign read: *No Unloading, 8 a.m. to 12 a.m.* Soon the stalled line of cars inched again toward the avenue, and Kennedy returned to the tête-à-tête.

"Somebody once said"—the mounted man's eyes twinkled—"that tomorrow never comes." He waved a newspaper clipping, then handed it down to Devereaux.

Devereaux took the clipping. It was a tear from a gossip column, *The Lyons Den*. It read: "Radio producer Travis Cord coaxing tough cop Johnny Devereaux out of retirement with $1,000-a-week offer as narrator on True Crime-File serial. Who said crime doesn't pay?"

"Big piece of change, a thousand per."

"I'm lighting out tomorrow," Devereaux said irritably. "Place your bet that way."

Kennedy grinned. "The offer will ride along with you. And in the end you'll find yourself sticking your hand out, hoping the offer still holds good."

"I don't need that much money." Devereaux scowled. "That much money is indecent." He closed his fist tightly and put the crushed clipping in his vest pocket. "Can I stay parked for a half hour?"

"All day, even." Kennedy chuckled. "I always give radio actors the run of the block."

"You go to hell."

2.

"Sorry," the clerk said, his eyes widening slightly at the sight of Devereaux. "She doesn't answer."

Devereaux looked into the small lobby. It was a family hotel, indeed, and despite Management's stern injunction against sterno cans and the single electric burner, an unmistakable odor of cooking hung in the atmosphere. The lobby loungers had the look of old residents, people to whom the broken chairs, shredding rugs, dust, and gloom were as familiar to their close, personal living as their next of kin.

"Maybe sitting out there somewhere?" Devereaux suggested.

The clerk peered. "No, she isn't."

Devereaux watched the clerk's fingers drum nervously

on the counter for a moment, then observed mildly, "Slick numbers depot. Smart boy."

"Wrong, Devereaux," the clerk protested. "You're dead wrong. I quit the racket."

"For clerking at thirty-five per?" Devereaux's lip curled derisively.

"It's a living," the clerk said.

"I'll bet! See Mrs. Gordon go out this morning?"

The clerk shook his head, then looked into a mail cubbyhole. "Funny," he said. "She isn't in, and she hasn't left her key." There was a small mystification in his face.

"Does she usually leave her key when going out?"

The clerk nodded, then looking earnestly at Devereaux, he said, "Going to jump at conclusions?"

"Know one reason why I shouldn't, with your record of arrests?"

"I'll lose my job." The clerk shrugged resignedly. "Okay, jump. I don't give a damn."

3.

The elevator stopped at the fourth landing. "Step up," the driver admonished.

Devereaux stood, watching the elevator until it dropped out of sight, then walked to a bend in the corridor where dirt-streaked windows opened into an airshaft. He found Room 418, and stood contemplating the door doubtfully. Momentary mystification in a room clerk's face hardly justified forced entry into a private citizen's hotel room.

He fingered a passkey, then flipped it into the air like a man tossing a coin. He caught the key and stooped to insert it into the keyhole.

Devereaux opened the door cautiously, closing it behind him, and then, as his eyes adjusted to the curtained gloom, the scene inside pulled together into a single, jolting effect. He looked hard, and again, as if expecting the scene to dissolve, while another scene, a more conventional one, appeared.

An elderly, gray-haired lady lay across a bed. Her eyes were fixed and unwinking, her lined features contorted. Dead, as if suddenly stricken. Devereaux's rapid examination revealed no weapon, no visible injury. Around her was the disorder of a hundred incidentals to ordinary living pulled from their grooves and left in an uncatalogued heap.

The detective roamed through the small, boxlike room. There were clothes, a reddish-tinged-with-gray hair switch, greeting cards marking the memory hoard of scores of years and as many occasions, papers, swatches of cotton and silk, rhinestone-studded hatpins of a bygone day, a St. James Bible standing on the floor like a motionless grasshopper.

A beaded handbag held a net of $8.36. Devereaux retrieved an article from the floor and turned it absently in his hand. It was an enameled piece, like a polished sea shell, reading "San Francisco Exposition, 1914." He picked the Bible off the floor and read the dedication page for a melancholy moment. An ink inscription, paled by time and set inside a flower design, read "To Cora Jennings, from Mother."

Devereaux nodded mechanically to himself. Cora Jennings. Undoubtedly the lady of Jennifer Phillips' reminiscence. He glanced toward the bed and his mouth pursed regretfully. A gray-haired lady, to be revered and buried sentimentally in the great family album. The scene before him was all wrong, with Cora Jennings atrociously miscast.

Devereaux went about the business of seeking out the less obvious evidences of assault and search. Corners, recesses, cubbyholes exposed nothing. Nothing of the assailant torn away in struggle, if there had been a struggle. No cuff link, button, strands of hair, bits of cloth, nothing. Fingerprints, if there were any, must wait on proper equipment.

Devereaux went to an only closet and peered inside. It

was pitch dark, and crammed tightly with clothing and luggage. He was feeling about blindly for a light switch, when the lights happened like an Independence Day rocket bursting inside his head.

Devereaux raised his guard, too late, then grappled wildly with a charging mass of flesh, but too weakly. His hands were dying, and a sudden knee in his groin started a nausea that rose to join the pain in his head. He clawed the air, and fell with dresses and coats raining on his head.

He came to with a colony of dwarfs working tiny hammers in his head. Then, off the floor and out from under the pile of clothes, he found the sink and stuck his head under a running faucet. When the colony of dwarfs was reduced to just one, Devereaux studied himself in a hanging mirror. There was a lump on his head where a blunt instrument, a blackjack undoubtedly, had struck his skull, and his cheek near the left eye sported a mouse that was rapidly becoming a clear shade of blue.

As he quit the room, he was acutely alive to the lingering pain in his groin. He took the stairs down, reached the lobby, and then, without breaking stride, signaled the desk clerk to follow him.

Devereaux entered a room whose sign read *Office*. A moment later, the clerk joined him.

The clerk surveyed Devereaux uneasily, his eyes noting details of the detective's battered appearance.

"I was slugged in Room 418," Devereaux said. The desk clerk met the detective's glare silently. "Got any ideas about who did it?"

The clerk shook his head.

Devereaux collared the clerk and pulled him close. "You've got sharp eyes and you don't miss a bet. No one crosses that lobby without being cased."

"I saw nobody," the clerk said.

Devereaux pushed him away. "Empty your pockets. Turn them inside out."

The clerk complied, then watched Devereaux finger through miscellaneous and commonplace items.

"Like I said, I'm not taking bets any more."

"Strip," Devereaux ordered.

The clerk looked at Devereaux protestingly. The detective's blow caught him just under the jaw, close to the Adam's apple. His hands were up defensively when the second blow bent him forward. Then, looking sick and green and tormented, the clerk began loosening his tie. Soon, nude except for a khaki money belt around his waist, he unbuttoned the belt sullenly and handed it to Devereaux.

Devereaux emptied its contents on a table. There were scores of small, square slips of paper—the day's numbers play of chauffeurs, shine boys, doormen, workers, sundry bettors in the area.

"I said you were a smart boy," Devereaux said.

The clerk stooped to recover his shorts and Devereaux kicked them out of his reach. "I asked you a question a while ago!" The detective disdained the mute appeal in the clerk's eyes. "Who did you see running out of that lobby?"

The clerk shook his head, then held his ground stubbornly as the money belt whacked across his mouth. He pressed fingers to the flow of blood from his underlip, with his eyes studying Devereaux as if detached from the pain he felt, as if speculating on the limits or extremes of the detective's relentlessness. Finally he said sullenly, "Nick Longo."

Devereaux looked at the clerk blankly. The name meant nothing to him. "Longo," the clerk repeated. "He's an old-timer."

"New to me." Devereaux frowned. His encyclopedic knowledge of the city's underworld was a matter of pride with him. Very few had eluded his ken, and when it happened Devereaux took it as a personal failure. "Unless the name's a phony," he said. "What does he look like?"

"Medium height, dark. Face looks like it's been through the mill."

"Jail?"

"How should I know?"

"What's his racket?"

The clerk shook his head. "I just happen to know the guy by name."

Devereaux looked at the clerk shrewdly. "How much did he throw you to play dumb?"

The clerk reddened. "Twenty bucks." He added hastily, "But just to forget I saw him."

4.

On the street, Devereaux made his way to a candy store-luncheonette. The pay-station phone booth was unoccupied. He entered and dialed.

"Police Headquarters," the voice announced.

Devereaux muffled his voice. "Check Room 418 at the Hotel Orleans."

"Who's calling?"

Devereaux kept silent, and the voice asked, "What happened there?" The detective hesitated irresolutely. Robbery, or attempted robbery, and possibly murder. But let the police see, satisfy themselves. For now he didn't want the events in Room 418 confused with the chore he had undertaken on behalf of a young lady. Not officially anyhow, not yet. He hung up and hurried to his car.

CHAPTER THREE

1.

The low building diagonally across from Bryant Park wore an outdoor sign on its brow that showed a shapely girl in a swim suit. The building, a pygmy in a skyscraper jungle, housed an odd variety of enterprises. Its directory listed, in part, a gypsy tea room, a check casher, a match-your-pants service, an Atheistic Pamphlet Press, a gold buyer, a schatchen, a diamond setter, a detective agency. The last, operated by a plump thirty-second-degree Mason, and a universally respected fellow to boot, was Devereaux's destination.

The gold lettering on the door read: *Solowey Detective Agency.* Devereaux smiled a secret, reverent smile as he took hold of the doorknob. Private detective Sam Solowey wore his badge like a clerical frock. A tolerant man, with the outlook of a psychiatric social worker, Solowey used his agency as an avenue to people and life.

The moon-faced, balding Solowey looked like a laughing Buddha. He was shoeless, and a giant toe peeked through a hole in one stocking. He wiggled his toe, greeting Devereaux, and put down his open copy of *Variety.*

"Still around, eh?" Solowey said.

Devereaux nodded glumly.

Solowey chuckled. "You were in a big hurry to see the world."

"Have your joke, huh. Then let's get down to cases."

"I've had my joke." Solowey stepped into his shoes. "Now cases?"

"Job of research mainly. Do it yourself, or put a man on it. I want you to check into a girl's parentage. Discreetly."

"Who's hiring me?"

Devereaux hesitated. "I'm hiring you."

Solowey stared at him shrewdly. "You, the retired detective! Come, I've got a first-aid kit in the washroom."

"I'm all right."

Solowey shook his head. "The hair should be cut away and the wound cleaned."

"First get a pencil."

"Go ahead, talk." Solowey held a pencil over a scratch pad.

"The girl's name is Jennifer Phillips. She's twenty. Martin Phillips is supposed to be her father."

Solowey's eyes grew round. "*The* Phillips?"

Devereaux nodded. "Find out where he was born, when married and to whom, what offspring if any. Everything. Is the assignment clear?"

"That much, yes." Solowey's lips pursed. "He is supposed to be her father, you said?"

"The girl thinks he's not, but with nothing actual to go on." Devereaux stopped. An involuntary wave of anger was surging through him. He felt Solowey's shrewd eyes reading his face, fathoming the depth of his emotion.

"You have a deep personal concern," Solowey observed quietly.

Devereaux nodded darkly. "From the girl's account, and what I guessed, the man's a sybarite, unnatural, an obscene and gilded pervert." His voice grated. "He pressed courtesan negligées on her at fourteen, whores' perfumes at fifteen."

Their eyes met and Solowey said, "It lends body to the rumors I have heard about Phillips."

"Rumors?" Devereaux's brows lifted.

Solowey nodded. "Ugly rumors, of a kind with those that

circulate about distinguished people. The many of them, of course, are false and malicious."

"Skip the tolerance preamble," Devereaux said impatiently. "What's the word on Phillips?"

"Homosexual."

Devereaux frowned but said nothing.

Solowey quit the room, then came back with scissors and a first-aid kit. "Sit," he commanded. The plump detective's hands worked busily. "You didn't report this assault on you."

Devereaux laughed. "Where do you hide your crystal ball?"

"Your insistence on discretion." The plump detective added pointedly, "The Solowey Agency license covers you."

Devereaux smiled his appreciation. "Odd thing is my retirement's still verbal. Final papers won't come through for thirty days. But thanks. It might be smarter to be your boy at that."

Solowey put the shears down, and commenced dabbing at the head wound with a wad of alcohol-soaked cotton. "Devereaux," he said in mildly chiding tones, "you should confide in a man you esteem enough to come to for help."

"In strict confidence," Devereaux stipulated, after a reflective pause.

Solowey's moon face went up and down solemnly.

2.

TAKE YOUR FORD BACK HOME, the sign said. Devereaux read it, then over again. It was a half mile away, across the city rooftops.

The Japanese manservant pattered up to the white-lacquered, wrought-iron terrace table, removed an emptied plate, and set a plate of berries down.

"Set another demitasse, Sato," the diner said softly, and resumed eating. After each completed mouthful, the diner looked up to scrutinize his visitor, while a scowl gathered over his eyes.

The face was pulpy, and here in the sun the raw flesh underneath burned through as if covered by but one layer of skin. It was sick-looking, degenerated by too many powders, creams, too much care.

Sato pattered in, set a cup before Devereaux, then poured for both of them from a gleaming silver pot. Phillips pushed the emptied plate of berries away, grasped his cup, and gestured abruptly at Devereaux The detective raised his cup and sipped. Sato came to clear the table in quick, efficient movements.

"Brandy, Sato," Phillips ordered.

Sato left with a trayful of soiled dishes, and Phillips sat back in that little ritual of siesta usual to gourmands with faulty digestion. Devereaux's eyes patiently searched out the Ford sign.

"Devereaux, you said your name was?" Phillips began at last, as if finally disposed to curiosity.

"Johnny Devereaux."

"And you're a policeman?" He said it as if it were a vexatious and incomprehensible thing.

Devereaux nodded smilingly.

"Go ahead," Phillips said in a discouragingly flat tone, as if it now devolved upon Devereaux to prove his sheer right to existence.

"Shouldn't have barged in this way," Devereaux said. "But it couldn't wait on formality. Homicide is like that."

"Homicide?" The eyebrows lifted mockingly.

"An elderly lady registered at the Hotel Orleans as Mrs. Minna Gordon." Devereaux looked closely at Phillips, watched little colored veins sprout in either cheek. The reaction was consistently in kind; Phillips' one evident emotion was that of a man bothered by an interloper.

"Shall I consult my lawyer?" The eyebrows lifted again.

"Perhaps," Devereaux said coolly. "If you have a feeling of guilt about something."

"I advise you not to badger me."

Devereaux said, "I'm just doing a job."

"What do you want of me?"

"A statement, of a kind."

"I'm suspected of murdering an elderly lady?" Phillips inquired incredulously.

"I didn't say that. If you'd just listen—"

"I'm listening."

"The lady was struck down by a prowler. Strangled or frightened to death or both. Pending a medical report, I don't know. The disorder in her room suggests that she didn't come to her death normally."

Phillips looked bored. "Please hurry it up."

Devereaux continued evenly, "My search of her belongings told me little of how she lived or what she did. There were mainly mementos that told about her life long ago, when she was younger, a young woman." The detective paused, his eyes sharply on Phillips. "I'm here for additional information about her."

"But why did you come here?"

"Never mind. Just tell me what you know about her."

"Nothing," Phillips said. "I never heard of a Mrs. Minna Gordon."

"Think again," Devereaux said in open disbelief.

Phillips looked disdainful. Devereaux watched Phillips' hands move nervously, saw the little colored veins sprout in his host's cheeks.

Devereaux said, "You never heard of her as Minna Gordon, perhaps. But her birth name in a St. James Bible was Cora Jennings."

Phillips reached his feet with the sudden force of a man bursting bonds. "You'll have to go," he said harshly.

Devereaux went to him and seized his arm. "The act isn't going over. Cora Jennings was in contact with you."

Phillips pulled his arm free angrily.

31

"The record at the Hotel Orleans switchboard shows the deceased phoned you many times." It was a lie, but told with compelling heat.

Phillips seemed to wilt for a minute, then the anger flamed again, burning away every other emotion that may have been in his face for Devereaux to read.

Sato came pattering up, and Phillips said harshly, "Show the gentleman out, Sato." He turned his back to Devereaux.

The temptation to manhandle this dandified and dissolute sensualist was overwhelming, but Devereaux turned away. He had walked a few irresolute steps in Sato's wake when he saw her.

Her face was pressed against the pane of a French window that opened on the terrace. Her look begged his strength, begged him to be sure in his method.

Devereaux made a furtive sign, reassuring her. He waited, hoping for a sign of her belief to show in her look; then, finding it, he walked rapidly in Sato's wake.

The door closed firmly behind him.

CHAPTER FOUR

1.

An hour had elapsed, and Devereaux's vigil yards away from the street door to Phillips' penthouse seemed time down the drain. He shifted restlessly in the cramped front of the Buick.

A miscalculation, this watch, he thought ruefully. Phillips, stung into an action by his sudden visit, might merely have resorted to the telephone.

Now dusk was falling with mid-September suddenness, and sharp details were blurring in the gathering night. Lights were appearing, rapidly becoming more numerous. Devereaux sighed and turned the ignition key. The motor was throbbing when the detective jerked to sudden attention.

He saw only the rear of the man moving briskly to a cab a yard below the canopy. But though this silhouette seemed leaner than the corseted figure on the terrace, and though it might have been a hundred strangers other than his quarry, Devereaux knew it to be Phillips surely. The eccentric slant of the black Homburg and the flailing walking stick could be only Phillips.

Devereaux smiled his satisfaction and guided the Buick in the wake of the taxicab.

The taxicab chewed through the jam of nighttime Second Avenue like a contestant in an obstacle race. Devereaux, stalled behind a beer truck and close to defeat in the chase, watched the taxi turn left against heavy traffic in a feat of split-second timing. Then, luckily, in the farthermost range of his vision, he saw the taxi stop at the curb, saw Phillips alight.

The light changed, and Devereaux made his left turn, then maneuvered the Buick into the nearest available curb space.

On the curb, he looked over Phillips' destination. It was the Attic Circus, a supper club with a special appeal to the sporting fraternity, owned by Lippy Latimer, bantamweight king of the twenties, now reduced to a restaurant, partial paralysis of the facial muscles, and weekend painting. The latter therapy, pursued with surprising doggedness by the ex-pugilist, had borne a one-man water-color show, winning not a few critical accolades. The nickname "Lippy" commemorated Latimer's ring technique of synchronizing boxing with an endless stream of withering invective. Whether the jabbering or the jabbing wilted the opponent, nobody could ever say for sure. One of them, if not both, had won Latimer the bantamweight crown. In losing the title, Latimer lost much of his power of speech. The challenger, a redoubtable puncher who was hard of hearing, shut Latimer up with a crushing blow on the nerve center. From then on, the nickname "Lippy" was more ironic than characterizing.

Like a great many New Yorkers, Devereaux knew Lippy, and like many of the initiate, he also knew and savored Lippy's cuisine.

Devereaux looked at his watch. Well past the dinner hour. Time for a songstress to materialize with the dishes of dessert. He looked at the sidewalk advertisement. The pouting mouth and nippled hills behind gauze were identified as "Sadye, Queen of the Double-Entendre."

Devereaux started into the club doubtfully. Anonymity was impossible, here where everybody came to see everybody else, and to be seen. Anonymity was especially impossible for a gadabout detective who'd just completed a twenty-year midtown roving beat and whose face was a front-page commonplace.

In the vestibule, the checkroom girl smiled brilliantly. "Good evening, Mr. Devereaux."

Devereaux kept his hat. The headwaiter's prop smile seemed a shade more genuine. "Mr. Devereaux." He bowed.

Devereaux eluded the headwaiter, then, spotting Phillips, moved quickly around the edge of the club to a position as distant from his quarry's table as he could get.

Phillips was huddled in whispered conversation with a companion. A waiter was removing emptied highball glasses and setting down another round. Devereaux felt a moment of surprise when he identified the waiter. Lippy, the owner himself, was doing the honors.

Lippy moved away, and Devereaux watched the pair, seeking an impression. They seemed steeped in an anxiety that absorbed them both. Was the other man a lawyer, summoned to meet Phillips, advise him? Devereaux considered it, then dismissed it, as he watched the tempo of their exchange mount in intensity. Plainly, from their expressions and manner, the men had a partnership in a problem that threatened them both equally.

His ruse had worked. The harried Phillips had hurried to a rendezvous. Devereaux studied Phillips' companion, seeking a mental picture that could be remembered. Middleaged, close in years to Phillips, ruddy-faced, kempt. There was nothing that distinguished him physically from the run of successful, and perhaps prosperous, executives.

"Eating or leaving, Devereaux?" The familiar sounds came from behind him. Sounds of speech pushed up from the larynx, without clear articulation.

Devereaux twisted to face the small, dapper ex-pugilist, and was at once aware of a difference in Lippy's manner toward him. A warmth and liking for him that he'd always

35

found in Latimer's eyes wasn't there, and Devereaux wondered about it.

"Dropped in to wash my hands, Lippy." Devereaux winked with the euphemism. "Okay?"

"Any time," Lippy said, and punched Devereaux in the stomach in a trade gesture he had never relinquished. "If a guy's gotta go—" He left the observation unfinished.

Devereaux went to a passageway that led down a short flight of stairs, puzzled by a feeling he couldn't shake that Lippy's eyes were burning into his back.

He came up from the club washroom with the first notes of Sadye's song. Lippy was where he had left him, against the far wall, with his eyes trained on the passageway leading to the washroom, like a sentinel on a fixed post.

Sadye nudged the diners with a melodic innuendo, and held her next lines until the guffaws subsided. Devereaux grinned across the room at Lippy, and joined in a round of applause. Sadye bowed revealingly, then resumed her song.

Devereaux waved to Lippy and left the club.

2.

Outside, and moving with purpose, Devereaux crossed the street, continued on for a few steps, then descended some basement steps to a store. Venetian blinds hid the interior and its activity from passers-by and peekers. Devereaux rapped on the door.

A girl opened the door warily, then, after identifying him with mild surprise, admitted him.

Inside, under stark fluorescent lights, the spots of rouge on her raised cheekbones had a lavender tone. She looked tubercular. Except for a couple of spindly chairs and some improvised shelves, the room was unfurnished. There was a scattering of photographic equipment on the shelves. A beaver-board partition in the back divided the small store into two compartments.

Her face was questioning him. Devereaux motioned her

36

toward the rear. "This couldn't be a pass, could it?" she said drearily, following him.

"Nice talk, Pearl," Devereaux said.

Pearl picked a box camera with a press photographer's bulb attachment on it off a shelf. "I gotta go take pictures," she said.

The idea of roving camera girls, begun as an experiment a decade earlier, had mushroomed into big business. Operators, located in bare stores strategically central to Manhattan's numerous Mazda Belts, cajoled, bought, or browbeat photographic concessions from night-club owners. The concessionaire's investment required a makeshift darkroom geared for speedy delivery of pictures, cameras, and peroxide blondes with a knack for melting consumer resistance. The girls worked on a percentage basis.

"There's a picture I want you to take," Devereaux said.

"Look, I'm not a policeman's little helper," Pearl said.

Devereaux smiled. Old in her youth, undoubtedly slumborn, and graduate of countless badger games and petty rackets, the girl was smarter than a woman should ever be. He reached into his pocket.

"For twenty?" Devereaux said.

She shook her head. "I've got twenty," she said.

"Sorry, I should have known better." Devereaux smiled. "How about for a cause?"

Her brow wrinkled, and the penciled eyebrows lifted.

"The guy's a bad actor," Devereaux said. "A very bad actor."

She shook her head. "Causes never got me."

A moment passed, with Devereaux looking futile. "How will I know the guy?" she said suddenly.

Devereaux brightened. "Two fellows at Table Nine, not far from the bandstand. One's ruddy-faced, plumpish, looks like a banker. The second's pretty well known. Phillips. Martin Phillips, the critic. No doubt you've seen him around."

"The queen," she said, curling her lip. "Why doesn't he go get psychoanalyzed?"

"On the sly, now," Devereaux admonished. "Don't get caught at it."

"You kidding?"

"Don't mind me. It's important, and I'm a little anxious." Devereaux looked gratefully at her. "For the record, kid, why are you suddenly doing it?"

"For you."

"This couldn't be a pass," Devereaux smiled.

"Devereaux, I read your book," she began mysteriously. "Twenty years a cop. And you never played favorites or took a crooked dollar, it says. So unless you were lying, that makes you Jesus Christ."

"Thanks," Devereaux said.

She slung the camera over her shoulder. "I like an honest man." She went to the door. "My father was an honest man."

CHAPTER FIVE

1.

The big hands worked over the neck muscles, then the back, then beat a climactic tattoo along the spine. Devereaux sat up, blinking contentedly with sun spots in his eyes and on his cheeks, then knotted a towel around his waist.

"Mister, what hands," he said admiringly, sliding off the table. "Hands like a sculptor."

The muscular Finn grinned over his hands, then punched Devereaux's midriff. "Loose, like a woman," he said reprovingly.

"Middle age," Devereaux said dolefully. "But I'll work it off," he promised.

"Now shower," the Finn ordered, enjoying his moment of eminence and authority.

Solowey came in and surveyed the scene wryly. Devereaux gestured the masseur out of the room.

"Nice place to conduct detective business!"

Devereaux smiled. "Peel and get massaged."

"I don't like massages," Solowey sniffed.

"Keeps you young."

"And I don't like youth. Too trying. The only thing I can remember about my youth is one big impatience to grow older." Solowey smiled. "A scholar once said, you grow old if you're lucky. I like being fifty."

"Then comes sixty," Devereaux shuddered.

"First comes fifty-one."

Devereaux shook his head. "After fifty you count by tens."

"And that scares you, eh, Devereaux?" Solowey looked at him shrewdly. "My good friend, I wouldn't exchange a precious minute of age for an hour of youth. Or a small idea for the muscles of a strong boy. You believe me?"

Devereaux nodded mechanically. "Why not?"

"Then also believe me when I say"—Solowey's eyes sought and held Devereaux's—"that this obsession you have with gymnasiums and athletics is a lack of maturity I have long detected in you." Solowey sighed. "Forty-one, with all the painful triumphs you have won over foolishness, and you would surrender it all just to be twenty."

Devereaux frowned. "Pretty broad generality, no?"

"Is it? At forty-one, already a retired detective. Like you were seventy. And running away somewhere, in search of yesterday. Now, in your best season. Now, when you are at the peak of your usefulness."

"Talk, talk." Devereaux went to the shower stall. "Best way to shut you up is to drown you out." The shower hissed into life.

Later, while Devereaux dressed, Solowey chuckled over an open newspaper. "This clever Phillips. So clever, and such a misanthrope. Listen to his paragraph about an opening last night." Solowey read, " 'The theatrical season opened last night to prove once again that innocuousness is a special virtue of the human species. *Safe Harbor* made its point admirably. Take it away, Hollywood.' "

Devereaux made a face. "What about Phillips' background? Find out something about him?"

"Very little, my friend." Solowey shrugged. "Two men worked all day producing a blank page. An expensive day, and for nothing. Libraries, newspapers, colleagues, nothing. Phillips is a man without a past."

"Exactly how much of his past is obscure?"

"Everything until a book of criticism published ten years ago. After the book, Phillips began to become somebody. About Phillips, the critic and essayist, there is much. There are articles about him, newspaper pieces, but no personal information, no background. It's like Phillips was born with the first book he published."

"No record of a marriage?"

"We haven't found one yet. About the daughter, except for one picture printed in *Harper's Bazaar* three years ago, also no record."

"What was the occasion for the picture?"

"A horse show given by a New City, Rockland County, Country Club. Phillips and the girl were in riding habit. The caption read, 'Martin Phillips and his daughter, Jennifer.' I'm having a photostat made for the files." Solowey made a gesture. "Anyhow, my men are still searching."

Solowey turned some pages back from the theater page of his newspaper. "Also, Devereaux, a few changes were made in that story you told me yesterday." He tapped a news column.

Devereaux arrested the knotting of his tie and craned toward the newspaper. "That old lady wasn't murdered," Solowey said. "A heart attack was the cause of death."

Devereaux frowned thoughtfully and Solowey continued, "And nothing was stolen, according to the police. Nothing they could determine, anyhow. A sum of money, about six hundred dollars, some trinkets, a watch, and some antique jewelry weren't touched."

"But the room was sacked."

"Sacked, yes. So Longo was looking for other things, maybe, when he hid in that closet."

Devereaux's eyes widened. "How do you know it was Longo!"

"I found out the same way you did. But with far less violence." Solowey smiled. "Like you, I guessed a man with sharp wits must also have sharp eyes. So I questioned the room clerk. He was first reluctant, but he finally talked without too much persuasion."

"After I softened him up," Devereaux said grimly.

"Perhaps." Solowey caught Devereaux's eye. "Another curious need in you, my friend. This need to be a tough cop. That was a pretty savage beating you gave the hotel clerk."

The implication irked. "The city's a lot cleaner for my twenty years of being a tough cop, Solowey."

"Cleaner, perhaps. But is it a lot wiser?"

"Look," Devereaux began irritably, "violence is the only language hoodlums understand."

"There are ways better than fists, my friend. Far better ways. Every time you use your fists, Devereaux, you lose something. You prove that you're a tough cop, sure. But you prove something else, too."

"Prove what?" Devereaux frowned.

"Another time, maybe, I'll dare tell you." Solowey smiled. "Meanwhile, one favor I ask. Don't turn the room clerk in."

"But he's taking numbers bets."

"A little cog in a big wheel. You should arrest the bankers, Devereaux."

"I caught the room clerk," Devereaux said grimly.

"He has a wife and a four-months-old infant."

"The man's a habitual offender."

"He'll quit, Devereaux. He took an oath with me."

Devereaux shook his head. "He's lying."

"Perhaps. But a man who swears to God should be believed once, and maybe even once again. Being believed helps a man develop self-respect."

Devereaux shook his head. "No good, Solowey. I'm not playing judge and parole officer. Never have, never will. I'm a cop, and an arrest is an arrest."

Solowey sighed. "You make me think just a little bit less of you, my friend."

"What does this Mrs. Jennings, or Mrs. Gordon look like?"

Devereaux pursed his lips. "What do you know about Nick Longo?" he said after a while.

"Next to nothing. A subway pickpocket, from what I know. We're checking further."

Devereaux got into his coat, then reached into an inside pocket. "Drop Longo, for now. I'll go after him." He held a photograph out. "Know the man seated with Phillips?"

Solowey said, "No. But if I had time—"

"You've got all morning, at least. What would you say went on at that table, from the expressions in the picture?"

Solowey said promptly, "Thieves huddled together. They've reached some crisis and are conferring on strategy."

Devereaux nodded. "My impression exactly. Phillips hurried to meet the other fellow after I shot a little fear into him."

They quit the room, went down a short corridor, then entered the main artery of Slattery's Gym for Men. To the quick glance, the vast room looked like a frenzied free-for-all. Men of every size, in shorts of every color, were huffing, snorting, feinting, shadow-boxing, while their managers and trainers watched them with the weary look of men gone dopey from gazing into crystal balls.

"They're learning," Devereaux observed. "And somewhere in this room is a champion."

"They're learning how to walk on their heels," Solowey said.

In a corner ring, a hairy fellow was doing a successful imitation of the Dempsey crouch and weave, until a blow on the ear hung him on the ropes.

"That'll save him pain later on," Devereaux said. "The Dempsey style's not suited to him. Arms are too short."

"It's a lunatic asylum." Solowey looked about him disgustedly. "When they could be spending their time in the public library—" He left the sentence unfinished, and hurried to the exit in advance of Devereaux.

The teletype commenced its animated click, click Devereaux snapped forward to scan the sheet.

"Ninety per cent of you never left the force, Johnny." The wiry man at the desk made no attempt to conceal his amusement.

"I was hooked into this one, Anders," Devereaux said. "First chance I get, I'm still shoving off."

Captain Anders laughed shortly. "You'll throw your neck out of joint. Better let me read it to you." He tore the sheet from the machine. "Nick Longo. Age, 48. Olive complexion, aquiline nose. Height, 5'6". Weight, 148 pounds. Scar tissue on neck under left ear. Specialty, pickpocketing New York subway system. Nine arrests to 1945. No convictions. Convicted of felony, 1946. Sentenced to Sing Sing for two and a half years."

Devereaux showed surprise. "Nine arrests for pickpocketing and no convictions?"

"It happens." Anders shrugged. "Shrewd article. Clever mouthpiece, maybe." He looked up. "Sure Longo's your man?"

Devereaux nodded. "What was the felony that got him time up the river?"

"Murtagh's in the file room on it now. If you'll just sit tight."

Devereaux took the teletyped page and turned it in his hand thoughtfully. "Any room for doubt about how Mrs. Minna Gordon died?"

"None. Medical report was unqualified. It was a heart attack."

"Induced by shock," Devereaux said. "Longo's presence in her room brought it on."

"Maybe. But the medical fact is the heart was about to give up. A tire blowout in the street or a loud knock on the door could have done it, too." Anders shook his head. "Burglary or attempted burglary is the most you've got on Longo—*if* you can place him in that closet beyond any reasonable doubt."

"Burglary and assault," Devereaux said, touching his head reminiscently.

"Placing him in that closet might not be easy, Johnny. You've only placed him in that lobby of the Hotel Orleans. And that on the word of a numbers bookie."

The door opened, and a man in shirt sleeves carrying a folder loafed in. He said listlessly, "On Longo, Captain."

"What was that 1946 felony conviction, Murtagh?" Anders asked.

"Sullivan Law. Caught toting a gun."

"Okay, leave the file." Anders watched his aide leave, then turned to Devereaux. "There it is."

"Funny, huh?" Devereaux said after a reflective pause.

"What's funny?"

"That first conviction. A professional dip carrying a gun!"

"It happens."

"Doesn't jibe with the shrewd fellow who beat nine arrests."

Anders shrugged. "Still, it happens."

Devereaux looked sharply at Anders. "Criminals stick to a habitual pattern, Anders. Killers tote rods, con men dream up new swindles. Petty thieves stay petty, and pickpockets stick close to what they know best. I don't think I've found a single variation in twenty years."

"Maybe." Anders looked thoughtful. "Then Longo's the exception to the rule. He did attempt burglary in that hotel room, you say. That was off the beaten path for a dip."

Devereaux nodded agreement. "Read me the file on that Sullivan Law rap."

Anders opened the folder and read it silently for a while. "Not much to it. Routine vagrancy arrests, and Longo was one of a crowd. When frisked, Longo was carrying a gun."

"Where was he picked up?"

"Outside the Paddock Café, up near Forty-ninth. Sergeant McClintock grabbed him. McClintock's on the Broadway squad." Anders pawed the air. "Guilty plea, and two and a half years in the Big House, period." He closed the folder, looking at Devereaux curiously. "Now what are you looking perplexed about?"

"It's crazy."

"It's one and one. Longo's luck ran out."

"A small-time pickpocket carrying a gun!"

"Maybe he was ambitious for bigger things."

"A dip exposing himself outside a place as public and central as the Paddock Café?" Devereaux looked at Anders reproachfully. "Think for a minute. Ask yourself: what happens when a known pickpocket is seen hanging around Broadway?"

The answer came promptly. "He's pinched."

"On sight?"

Anders nodded.

"Then just being outside the Paddock was risky for Longo, a man with a long record of arrests. And a gun in his jeans made it fifty times riskier. Longo was inviting disaster."

Anders pondered briefly. "Okay," he acknowledged finally. "So Longo stepped out of character that day in front of the Paddock. And he was off base when you met him in that hotel closet. What does it add up to?"

"I don't know." Devereaux paced the room. "You said Longo got a two-and-a-half-year sentence. How long did he serve?"

Anders opened the folder, scanned it, then turned a page. "Served only fourteen months and then was paroled." He looked up. "Place him in that closet, and you've got him for violation of parole for a starter."

"Who sponsored his parole?"

Anders leafed through the folder. "Doesn't say here. Is it important?"

"Anything could be important."

"Okay," Anders sighed. "I'll get on the damned phone again." He opened a desk drawer, then held a cigar out to Devereaux. "Meanwhile, you chew on this. Calm down, and stop pacing the goddam floor." He mopped his brow. "You're getting me nervous."

CHAPTER SIX

1.

Water Street and its environs was a derelict mass of rust and broken brick just a hoot away from Manhattan's super-built financial district.

The Buick nosed slowly through the narrow labyrinth of streets, and soon eased to a stop. Devereaux alighted and stood regarding a wide, low building whose façade showed long neglect. Its store-front window sported the expensive beveling of another era, with elaborate designs tooled into the thick plate glass. A saloon once, he guessed, in the long-ago heyday of the Bowery. A barely legible sign read: OLD NEW YORK MISSION. Hand lettering on a dirty square placard propped inside the plate glass stated: SERVICES 5 P.M. COFFEE FREE. EVERYBODY WELCOME.

A man with unhealed sores on his nose and cheeks shambled up to Devereaux. "Watch your car?" he asked.

Devereaux shooed him away, crossed the sidewalk, and entered the Mission.

It was furnished like a meeting place. Benches in rows, and in the rear a platform and a rude pulpit. Battered hymn books were piled in neat rows on both sides of the platform. Except for two bums stretched across as many benches, in deep sleep, the room was deserted.

Devereaux cupped a hand to his mouth. "Hel-loo-oo."

The echo held lingeringly, and then he was aware of a sound overhead. Thump, thump, like kicks on the ceiling.

He listened, and the thump, thump was repeated. It sounded more like a cane now, striking the same section of the floor, as if signaling a response to his call. Devereaux waited, and soon there were footsteps overhead, the heavy tread of a heavy person moving across the floor.

Seconds later, the tread sounded on rickety wooden stairs that connected the two floors. Soon a man emerged from the gloomy side hallway. The shaggy gray mass of hair looked long unbarbered and uncombed. He was cadaverous, but in curious disproportion. The upper half of the frame had the overdevelopment of a heavyweight wrestler. What was below the top mass seemed spindly, almost delicate. He was carrying a heavy, black-lacquered stick for walking support.

The man stared near-sightedly as he moved closer to Devereaux. He stopped and furrowed his brow inquisitively.

"Maxim Buloff?" Devereaux asked.

The man made an affirmative sound in his throat.

"I'm Devereaux, a policeman. I've some questions to ask about a man you're interested in."

Buloff looked his question silently. "Longo. Nick Longo. You stood for him with the parole board," Devereaux said.

Buloff crooked a finger admonishingly, and turned away. He approached a bench and rapped a sleeper's ankles with his cane, then went to the second bench.

When the sleepers had blinked awake, cursed at their unfeeling host, then shuffled out of the Mission, Buloff turned the bolt in the door. He came back to confront Devereaux.

"You're from the probation office?" he asked.

"No." Devereaux watched Buloff's stare of surprise, then said, "Why did you stand for Longo, sponsor him?"

"To help him."

"A pickpocket and a convicted felon?"

"A man who begged for help." It was said with grave, ministerial dignity. "A human being, Mr. Devereaux," he added, as if this observation cut across the heart of the question and disposed of it.

"I know." Devereaux nodded impatiently. "But sponsoring a lawbreaker is quite a responsibility to assume." He looked at the premises disapprovingly, then trained his look on the eccentric detail of Maxim Buloff's whole appearance. "What possible check could you keep on Longo? What guarantee of his behavior?"

"His pledged word, Mr. Devereaux."

"You're being naïve, if I may be blunt."

Buloff looked offended. "The man has reformed, under my shepherdship." There was an uncompromisingly stubborn note.

"I'm sorry, Buloff. You sold the parole board the bill of goods you obviously first sold yourself. Longo's promise of reform was just talk, a way out of jail." Buloff looked disbelieving and hostile, and Devereaux said summarily, "The man's back in business. Criminal business, as usual."

"You can prove that?"

"Where's Longo?"

Buloff ignored the question, and Devereaux's tone sharpened. "Longo's under your wing, according to the terms of the parole, and lives here, or should. I order you to produce him."

A tense silence fell, like a deadlock, with Buloff in evident self-debate. Finally he said, "The man was not to be harassed. That was also a condition of my custody."

"I've got to question him," Devereaux said flatly.

Buloff looked defiant and his lips made muttering sounds that were lost to Devereaux's ears, but he motioned the detective to follow him.

"Torment the man and I give back my custody." The tones were growling. "I can't work with a man whom the police continue to persecute."

They entered the connecting hall and climbed the staircase in tedious single file. The narrow hallway was fraught with sickening odors.

The one room on the upstairs floor held an irregular arrangement of unmade beds, six in number, and an odd assortment of household appurtenances. The room was evidently a kind of dormitory, with kitchen facilities, of a sort, and other living comforts flung here and there into the disorder. Off in one corner, a broken screen failed to hide a gas range covered with the stains of many years of cooking. Several tavern-type tables, some covered with oilcloth, were scattered planlessly about the room. There were some chairs barely serviceable, a few kerosene lamps, magazines, odds and ends.

The room held two occupants. One, a middle-aged woman with prominent features, had the unmistakable look of a menial. She was carefully folding towels that looked newly washed, but without the use of a bleaching agent. The other was a man of medium height, with a swart complexion and an aquiline nose. He was sitting on a bed, staring about him emptily, like a man half-awake.

"Anna," Buloff called out gruffly, "go downstairs."

Anna folded the last towel methodically, then went to the staircase. Buloff beckoned to the man sitting on the bed and motioned both Devereaux and the approaching man to take chairs flanking a tavern table.

The man took a seat, first averting his gaze, as if preparing his face; then his eyes settled on Devereaux uneasily. The worry and alarm he felt was plain to see. The facial muscles twitched, like a tic, and the eyes showed fear.

Devereaux began with piercing directness. "I'm a policeman, Longo. And I'm also the man you laid out in a room in the Hotel Orleans."

Longo shook his head, as if erasing Devereaux from the view before him.

"Lying won't help, Longo," Devereaux continued coldly.

"I've got you dead to rights, and you'll just force me to beat the truth out of you."

Longo looked at Buloff appealingly, and the Mission head turned protestingly to Devereaux. "You'll shut up and not butt in, Buloff," the detective warned.

Devereaux coiled sudden fingers around Longo's wrist. "Buloff can't help you, so don't look for it. And if you've got an idea that this place is a haven, give it up, because I'll hustle you out of here so fast it will make your head spin."

The tic was alive in Longo's cheeks. Buloff said, "Tell the truth, Longo."

"What were you doing in that hotel room?" Devereaux asked.

Longo looked away from Buloff. His face had the shamed look of a child pushed to confess a misdeed. "I heard a noise at the door, and I hid in the closet."

The sudden distress in Buloff's face seemed genuine to Devereaux's quick estimate. The detective said, "That wasn't my question. I asked, what were you doing in the room?"

"I went in looking for money, jewelry."

"Into an occupied room?" Devereaux's tone rejected it. Longo stared at the detective blankly, and Devereaux said, "Even an amateur hotel thief knows enough to make sure the tenant is out before breaking in."

Longo said, "I thought the room was empty," as if he couldn't understand the significance of this line of discussion.

"What made you think so?" Devereaux persisted.

"I knocked, then hid in a turn in the hall and watched. Nobody came to the door. Then I let myself in."

"How?"

"With a master key."

Devereaux contemplated Longo. "How long had you been looting hotel rooms, before this job?"

Longo hesitated. "Two, three weeks," he finally said, glancing remorsefully toward Buloff.

The revelation seemed to stun Buloff. Devereaux watched the wild gray mane move back and forth dolefully, then resumed his inquiry. "Quite a switch for an old dog, huh? What made you decide on a new trick?"

Longo's eyes shadowed. "The police were arresting me on sight. I was too well known in—the old business."

"But you'd gotten by as a pickpocket for more than ten years. Not one conviction."

Longo smiled faintly, in a bare glow of pride. "Long time," he said in scarcely audible tones. "Long time, and too old." He held a hand out. "Hands no good any more." The hand was trembling badly. The dexterity needed for picking pockets was plainly lost to Longo.

Devereaux said, "So you let yourself into the hotel room with a master key. Go on from there."

Longo looked at Devereaux uncertainly. "I want an account of what happened inside, step by step," the detective explained.

"It was dark inside, and for a minute I didn't see her lying on the bed. I was at the bureau, when she made a sound. A sick sound, like someone who was hurt. I watched her try to get up, and then fall back. She lay there, breathing hard and choking and calling to me with her fingers. I went over to her, and watched her eyes close. I thought she had fallen asleep."

"It didn't occur to you that she might be dead?"

Longo shook his head. "Not until after I left."

"You went through the room before leaving. What did you take?"

"Nothing. I searched, but I didn't feel right with her lying there on the bed." It sounded curiously as if Longo were ashamed of his ungallant role in the hotel room. The thief shrugged, throwing off the mood. "There was nothing, anyhow. Eight dollars in the handbag. Cheap jewelry."

Devereaux grinned slightly. "*And* six hundred dollars hidden under the mattress, which we both missed. Go on."

"That's all. When I went to leave, I heard a noise at the door, so I hid in the closet."

"Blackjack in hand, and ready," Devereaux said grimly. Longo kept silent, and the detective asked, "How did you come to pick that particular room?"

"Just—" Longo shrugged, and left the reply unfinished.

"Like that, out of a hat?" Devereaux's eyes searched the thief's face. "Just coincidence that we both had business in the same hotel room, at practically the same time?"

"Just a bad break I got," Longo said. "I tried a room on the fourth floor first. I knocked, but somebody came to the door."

"Did you know who occupied the room you entered?"

Longo shook his head.

Devereaux twisted slightly, and brought both Longo and Buloff into simultaneous focus. "Know Martin Phillips?" he asked.

Longo's eyes widened slightly, and he shook his head.

"Answer the question, in English," Devereaux said with sudden sharpness.

Longo's eyes grew wider. "I never heard of him," he said emphatically.

Devereaux's eyes glinted at Buloff. "Do you know Martin Phillips?"

"No." Buloff sounded mystified. "Of what importance is this Martin Phillips?"

"How is this Mission of yours set up, Buloff?" Devereaux said irrelevantly.

"I don't understand." After a pause, Buloff added, "I have a charter."

"You're classified as a private corporation, devoted to welfare work?"

"Yes."

"Tax exempt?"

"Yes."

"Who conducts services?"

"I do."

"Are you an ordained minister?"

"No. I do not emphasize religion." An amused look flickered in Buloff's face. "My interest is rehabilitation and reform, chiefly."

"Where do the funds come from? How do you support the Mission?"

"I have some money of my own. I also solicit contributions."

"Keep books?"

Buloff nodded irritably.

"Your list of donors available for examination?"

"Of course." Buloff bridled. "Why these questions?"

"Nothing special."

"The proper affidavits were filed with the parole board. I do everything openly."

"I'm not questioning that." Devereaux looked at Buloff curiously. "One impertinent question?" he asked archly.

Buloff reddened. "If you must ask it!"

"Thanks." Devereaux smiled. "Why are you in this activity? Especially if, as you say, you aren't actuated by purely religious motives."

Buloff was silent for a while. "I believe in man's dependency on his brother."

"That's another way of saying religion, isn't it?"

"No. My idea differs. I believe this dependency is born of guilt. We all share a universal guilt. And from it we each take our measure of pain and suffering."

"Still a religious concept to me."

"Religion offers expiation and atonement, Mr. Devereaux."

"Don't you?"

"No, I don't." There was a new, harsh quality in Buloff's tones. "The pain is ever-present. Through all of physical life. Without relief or end."

"All seems a little hopeless, no?"

"Hope is a delusion, Mr. Devereaux. Our guilt increases with each day we live."

Devereaux motioned about him. "Then this derelict living, this wormy and uncomfortable setup, and the philosophy you bring to it—it's a kind of hell, huh?"

Devereaux flashed a look at Longo. The thief seemed uninterested in the discourse. The detective said, "Then there was no idea of reform really in your sponsoring Longo's parole. He was just to come live in this hell of yours."

Buloff said forbiddingly, "Longo believes in my word."

Devereaux turned to Longo. "Do you, Longo?"

"Sure," Longo said without conviction.

Devereaux looked at Buloff critically. "But Longo broke his word to you, and also broke his parole. What's your attitude on that?"

"His guilt is greater, and he consequently suffers more."

"I mean, would you still sponsor his parole?"

Buloff shrugged. "That is up to the police now."

Devereaux kept silent, weighing the substance of his inquiry, deliberating his future course. Was there a tie between Buloff and Longo, a tie other than the patent one of sponsor and parolee, he wondered. He felt Buloff's eyes vigilantly upon him. The volatile Mission head was a man of obviously secret depths, an enigma with twists in his character that required more than mere questions and answers to penetrate.

The detective looked at Longo, watched the chastened thief rolling and unrolling the end of his necktie. Arrest the ex-pickpocket turned hotel-room thief now? Devereaux debated. Do it as a routine arrest, dismissing the suspicious coincidence of Longo's presence in the same room he, Devereaux, had gone to on behalf of Jennifer Phillips? Or was Longo free, but under surveillance, the more logical way until the coincidence was proved or exposed?

"Longo," Devereaux began reflectively, waiting for the thief's attention. "How did you come to be carrying a gun that night in front of the Paddock Café?"

The hand working the end of the necktie stopped suddenly, and Longo seemed to go rigid.

"I haven't got all day," Devereaux said.

"I"—Longo was having difficulty finding his voice—"I must have been crazy."

Devereaux stared at the thief intently. "Queer that a known pickpocket would show himself along Broadway. And even more queer that he should be armed."

"I must have been crazy."

"It was like asking for a stretch up the river."

Longo nodded. "I was out of my head."

"You said you'd been rifling hotel rooms for several weeks. Where do you keep the loot?"

"I got rid of it."

"All of it?"

"All of it."

Getting Longo to disgorge loot, if there was any loot, would plainly require a more strenuous method than talk. "Where do you keep your baggage around here?" Devereaux asked.

Longo pointed in the direction of a bed.

"Get it and bring it here," Devereaux ordered.

Longo complied with unexpected alacrity.

Beyond soiled shirts, socks, shaving gear, incidentals, a search of the valise exposed nothing of incriminating nature. Devereaux pushed the valise away, and began to retreat toward the staircase.

"You're not pulling me in?" Longo asked incredulously.

"Not at this time," Devereaux smiled. "Why take you out of Hell and give you a nice, clean cell?" At the top of the staircase, he admonished, "But don't go anywhere."

Later, in a phone booth just around the corner in

Macauley's Old Saloon, Solowey's deep voice came over the earphone.

"Yes?"

"Put a twenty-four-hour watch outside the Old New York Mission, Solowey. And give your man a working description of Longo."

"Good."

"Got anything for me?" Devereaux asked.

"Yes."

"Then come see me sometime after five. I'll be home getting changed. Oh, yes, check the certificate of incorporation of the Old New York Mission at the Hall of Records."

"Good."

"Hurry that operative, Solowey. I'll keep watch until he gets here." Devereaux hung up, then paused holding a coin to the slot undecidedly. Phoning Jennifer Phillips at home meant taking a risk. There might be other ears or a house party wire.

Devereaux deposited the coin and began to dial. He'd take that risk.

CHAPTER SEVEN

1.

She was cream-cheeked, but even more so than in their first meeting, and she wore a tunic suit that enhanced her slender, youthful appeal. Devereaux felt his blood grow warm. And as once before, he was surprised at her effect on him.

"Brave of you to come," he began a little foolishly, then stopped.

She saw him flush, then joined in his forced, nervous laughter. With the merriment still in her voice, she said, "In the spider's web, and am I the brave, bold fly," and Devereaux continued to feel foolish.

"I'm a bachelor of long standing," he said with a candor that rang false to his ears, "and female visitors are sensationally rare." He turned and pointed around the room, as a way of hiding his face. "Look around. Not a feminine touch anywhere."

Now she was before him, her eyes brightly on him, enjoying his confusion.

"There's a lot of the teasing little girl in you," Devereaux said.

"And you're so much small boy," she said.

He led her toward a chair, feeling oddly grateful for this description of him. It bridged the gap of years between them, and brought him closer to her beauty and her youth.

His hand lingered lightly on her arm, and as her eyes smiled into his, he felt her magic at once in his fingers and on the tips of his ears.

He withdrew his hand hastily. No good, he told himself. No good chasing illusions. She was beautiful, and had what it took to touch off a kind of panic inside him he hadn't experienced for longer than he liked to remember, but it was no damned good. The girl was still wet behind the ears.

"All I need is an ice-cream cone in my hand," Devereaux said, making a face.

Her eyes wouldn't let go, and Devereaux said accusingly, "Hey, you're flirting."

Her eyes narrowed at the corners slightly, as if weighing the accusation. "If I am, it's nice," she said childishly, tilting her face closer to his.

"I'm older than God," Devereaux said solemnly.

She smiled his admission into discard.

"I creak getting out of bed mornings," Devereaux insisted desperately. Her smile dismissed that, too, and now there was a look growing in her eyes that he knew he had to stop, and quickly.

"Kid, I just retired after giving a lifetime to a job. I'm double your age." His voice died. There was a blur before him, and her face seemed to be wavering, and there were magnetic fingers pulling him to her. . . .

It was longer than he'd ever known a minute to be.

He drew away from her mouth. "Someone ought to lock me up," he said huskily.

Her eyes were lighted, and her face was shining. "I've got a crush on you," she said with her voice marveling.

"You've got a touch of hero worship," Devereaux said, making a decision about the mood that had plainly taken hold of her. "You've been falling for my publicity."

She shook her head. "I've got a crush on you," she insisted, now with just a trace of petulance.

"You're mixed up, kid. You're just looking for a protector."

She frowned, disavowing it, but unconvincingly. The detective grinned at her, and as he felt his self-possession returning, he breathed heavily in relief. A charming but idiotic interlude had been successfully contained. The kiss had been an irrelevant, if unforgettable, thing.

"Now, sit down," he said bluffly, feeling renewed mastery over himself. "We've business to talk over." He pressed sure fingers to her, pushing her into a seat, and suddenly his fingers and the tips of his ears were at once hot, as before.

He retreated across the room, and found a chair. The interlude, and the girl, hadn't been successfully contained. Proof, the electric currents charging through him, the bells in his head.

"Kid," he began after a while, taking himself in hand, "You've got an appeal for me, and I concede that. And it would take just a little push for me to horse myself into believing I'm a boy again." Devereaux smiled weakly. "I guess even Grandpa has a touch of the juvenile somewhere in him." A lecturing note came into his voice. "But that's not going to happen. I won't let it happen, and you're not to let it happen. I'll back out of your problem, and boot you out of my thinking, if that's the only way we can keep from getting silly." He looked across the room and held her eyes. "Okay?"

Her eyes looked misty, and her mouth seemed to tremble. She nodded and said, "Okay."

"Good." Devereaux's tones became businesslike. "Now, what was Phillips like when I left him yesterday?"

"He was strange. I'd never seen him in such a mood."

"Worried over my visit, what I'd said to him?"

She nodded. "And more than worried—frightened." She repeated, "Frightened."

"What did he do?"

"He made a hurried phone call."

"Do you know to whom?"

She shook her head.

"Overhear anything?"

"No. He has a private wire in his study. Besides, I wouldn't dare—overhear."

Devereaux said, "The number I reached you at—is it a house phone?"

She nodded.

"Is there a party wire hooked up to it?"

"No. And you needn't worry." She smiled. "I did it like a detective would. I took precautions against being overheard. And when I came here, I looked to see if I was being followed."

"Smart girl," Devereaux said approvingly. "I like you better as alert as this."

"Better than what?" she asked, wrinkling her forehead.

"Better than the panicky little jackrabbit you were that first night." He smiled. "Or is it jillrabbit?"

"Am I in danger?" she asked unexpectedly.

"Why do you ask that?"

"I don't know. It's just a feeling I have." She hesitated, then added quietly, "I know about Cora Jennings. I saw it in the papers." Her eyes sought Devereaux's. "The papers said heart attack, but could it have been murder?"

"No. I thought so for a while, but no. There was a prowler in her room when she died, but she died of natural causes." Devereaux looked intently at her. "Ever see or hear of a petty thief named Longo?"

She shook her head. "What does he look like?"

"Medium height and weight. Swart complexioned. Has a long scar under his chin running up to his neck. Maybe you saw such a man visiting Phillips?"

She shook her head positively. "Was he the prowler in Cora Jennings' room?"

Devereaux nodded. "Ever hear of a Maxim Buloff? Or the Old New York Mission?"

"No, never." She was as absorbed as a child in a puzzle. "What does he have to do with Cora Jennings?"

"He has to do with Longo. Buloff sponsored Longo's recent parole from prison. Longo lives in Buloff's Mission."

The puzzled look deepened in her face. "I don't understand. Those men, do they mean something?"

"I don't know," Devereaux frowned. "The Mrs. Minna Gordon who visited Phillips was the Cora Jennings of your recollection of early boarding school. And Longo was in her room, looking for something, when she dropped dead. It might have been sheer coincidence, with Longo there for petty theft, as he says, or—" Devereaux paused, shrugging. "*Or*, question mark. Deductions at this stage would only be guesswork. One thing, however. It looks like your suspicions about Phillips have more than fancied foundation. Your suspicions about his avowed relationship to you, I mean."

"You mean he's not really my father?" she asked hopefully.

"So far as I've gone, we've found no evidence of a marriage for Phillips. In fact, we've found no evidence of Phillips' existence beyond some years ago. No birth, no early beginnings." Devereaux smiled slightly. "It's as if he dropped into this planet a grown man." He looked at his wrist watch suddenly. "I've got to hustle you out of here. An associate is due any minute."

At the door, she said softly, "Thanks for all you've done."

"Save it for the final chapter, huh? I mean, *if* there's really a story, and *if* I'm lucky enough to write it." He looked into her face earnestly. "I don't want to alarm you, Jennifer. But you asked whether you were in danger, and I dodged answering your question. The fact is, I don't know. I don't know a damned thing yet. This much, however." Devereaux hesitated, seeking a suitable frame for his speech. "Your feeling about Phillips, your revulsion and your mistrust, whatever drove you to look me up, is your danger. So keep your eyes open, keep watchful, and be ready to make a run for it."

"Run where?" she said dismally.

"Anywhere. A hotel room. Run here, if you need to." He deliberated briefly. "Look, maybe you'd better run now. Not go back."

She thought it over. "No," she decided. "I'll go back. I may be able to help, if I'm there."

"Feel up to anything that might happen?"

"Yes. I'm not so afraid." Her mouth set firmly. "I'm not afraid any more," she said resolutely. "Not if you're here."

"Good girl." Devereaux smiled, opening the door. "We'll keep in touch."

She moved to pass him, paused, and pressed her lips to his cheek gratefully. Devereaux patted her on the head, then stood watching her move down the hall.

Trim, with the supple movements of a dancer, he thought regretfully. And as perfect as the curve of the moon. He watched her cross the vestibule and turn into the street. He must see her dance someday, he promised himself with a pang.

2.

Solowey stood posed just inside the door, looking like an obese and laughing Buddha. He worked his nostrils, scenting the air.

"Chypre, unmistakably. The delectable fragrance of morning." Solowey wagged a finger at Devereaux. "You'll lose your bachelorhood."

Devereaux grinned. "Didn't know you specialized in scents—and nonsense."

"Nonsense?" Solowey produced a handkerchief, moved forward with apparent aimlessness, then suddenly dabbed at Devereaux's mouth. "Shall we send it to chemical lab?"

"It didn't mean a thing." Devereaux found his handkerchief and rubbed the lip rouge off his mouth. "I've got twenty years on her," he said restlessly.

Solowey regarded Devereaux for a moment. "Age need

not be a barrier, my friend. Such marriages happen every day."

"And seniles crowd the front rows of burlesque houses. No good. In my book, youth goes with youth."

"Normally, yes." Solowey's hands gestured expressively. "But where do you find normalcy? People are driven by their needs. And this girl might need the security of a man just like you. A man in his prime. Experienced, resourceful—"

"Cut." Devereaux forced a grin. "You look like a cross between a fat Cupid and a marriage broker. Better start looking and talking like a detective, huh? What's new on Phillips?"

"Nothing. He's still a man without a past."

"Identify that photograph of Phillips' table companion?"

Solowey nodded and drew a small notebook out of his pocket. "No little fish, that other man. He is Frederick J. Castle, a wealthy and influential man."

Devereaux shook his head. "Never heard of him. What does he do?"

Solowey referred to his notebook. "He lives in a Summit, New Jersey, estate, and writes a weekly industrial analysis newsletter that circulates from Washington, D. C." A somber note crept into the portly detective's tone. "He also owns a publishing house that operates from Westlake under the name of Global Press."

Devereaux frowned. "Does that mean something?"

"Global Press was cited by the FBI for reprinting and circulating enemy propaganda during the war."

"Any result?"

"No. The charges were dropped. Global Press closed down, then resumed operations about a year ago." Solowey made a noise with his mouth. "The titles. You should read the titles."

"A rabble-rouser, huh?" Devereaux's brow corded in thought. "What links Castle and Phillips?"

"Bitterness, for one thing." Solowey's face showed distaste. "They bring the same cynicism to their separate fields."

Devereaux shook his head impatiently. "What can they worry over in common? Their fields are so utterly different."

"Their backgrounds are alike," Solowey said.

Devereaux said eagerly, "What do you mean?"

"Castle bought his Summit estate fifteen years ago, and settled there. But where he came from, what his antecedents were, nobody knows. We inquired around, did a little checking, but for nothing. Like Phillips, Castle seems to have no past."

Devereaux nodded approval. "You've done a lot in little time."

"A lot of expense," Solowey said doubtfully. "Being thorough but hurried means paying salaries and bonuses." He looked at Devereaux sympathetically. "Who is paying the bills?"

"I am, I guess." Devereaux tugged his wallet free and counted out some bills. "Three hundred, meanwhile. More tomorrow when I get to the bank."

"You're in love, my friend," Solowey said softly, pocketing the money.

"I'm a Boy Scout," Devereaux said. He looked at Solowey uncertainly. "If what we're about really spells the welfare of the girl. An ex-pickpocket turned hotel thief, a weird missionary, and now your Frederick J. Castle. How do they relate to the problem of a girl who thinks her father isn't her father?"

Solowey shrugged. "It's a mix-up."

"Check those articles of incorporation?"

Solowey nodded and referred to his notebook. "The Mission is bona fide; everything seems in order. The papers were filed over ten years ago. The officers of the corporation were listed as Maxim Buloff, Anna Aho Jorgensson, and Thomas Latimer."

66

"Anna Jorgensson," Devereaux said thoughtfully. "Might be the housekeeper. Buloff called her Anna." He stiffened, as if reacting to a sudden jolt. "Say!"

"Yes?" Solowey's eyes prodded Devereaux.

"Thomas Latimer! That's Lippy. Lippy Latimer. That sneak photograph of Castle and Phillips was taken in Lippy's Attic Circus."

"Interesting," Solowey began cautiously. "It could mean a great deal, and it could mean nothing."

"Lippy was unusually unfriendly that other night. Practically gave me the bum's rush," Devereaux said.

"Do you think he knew you were spying on Phillips' table?"

"I don't know." Devereaux's tone pitched excitedly, "But Lippy knew both Castle and Phillips. He was at their table, setting drinks down, playing host."

"You have added another actor to your cast. An ex-pugilist and restaurateur. Maybe they all relate, maybe not." Solowey shrugged. "So far you have not less than three investigations running."

"But we *have* established relationships. Phillips and the girl relate to the deceased Cora Jennings. And we can assume that Phillips relates to Castle, somehow. Buloff and Longo relate, and Latimer's name in those articles of incorporation relates him to Buloff. That gives us all of our principals in *two* not *three*, groups. Phillips and Castle, *one*. Longo, Buloff, and Latimer, *two*. And we can rationalize the two groups into one, on the basis of Latimer's presence at the Castle-Phillips table in the Attic Circus, and on the basis of Longo's presence in Cora Jennings' room."

Solowey was silent, mulling it over. "One circle, with the girl in the middle." He smiled wryly. "Makes an interesting pattern. It also makes for more checking. And more checking means more money." Solowey's smile deepened. "And if Latimer turns out to be a man without a past, like the others—"

Devereaux interrupted impatiently, "Forget Latimer for now. We've nothing on him or Castle or even Phillips. Nothing that even gives us a valid police excuse for questioning them. If I examine them, it will be strictly on my nerve. They can shut me up, throw me out, and undoubtedly know it."

Devereaux crossed the room, got a cigarette from a box set on a low coffee table, and lighted up. "You dig into Maxim Buloff," he resumed nervously. "And keep that watch on Longo. Something in that weird relationship stinks to high heaven, and the first break may well come from there—*if* we keep prying, if we follow the smell to its source." He stopped, drew a deep breath. The subtle scent of Chypre was still in the room.

"You're a scent detective, Solowey," Devereaux said. "Just follow your nose."

CHAPTER EIGHT

1.

The estate was a quarter mile past a large, well-kept cemetery, and enough out of Summit to be considered between towns. Night was lowering, and there were bells ringing somewhere. Devereaux slowed the Buick to a crawling pace, switched his headlights from dim to bright, then maneuvered the car into a grassy siding that formed a narrow island between a white picket fence and the country road.

The bells had died and now there were the eerie hoots of distant locomotive whistles as Devereaux started up a fieldstone walk. The big frame dwelling ahead of him was darkened. Nobody home, evidently, unless sudden night had preceded the turning on of lights.

He picked his way carefully, skirting the close sequences of flower beds and plants, then waited halfway up the walk, imagining eyes upon him and feeling uncomfortably conspicuous and exposed. A long minute passed, and no lights showed inside as the gloom outside grew heavier. Devereaux completed the rest of the path to the main door, grasped the ancient brass pull, and sounded the bell inside the house.

He waited, somehow tenser than necessary for the conventional thing he was doing, and with his senses acute to the sound inside as it traveled loudly through the lower floor and coursed upstairs, to die away in the higher reaches of the house.

Damn darkened houses in the country, he swore silently. He found a cigarette, lighted it, and looked at the bulking frame dwelling speculatively. It was a new and strange environment for a man weaned on auto horns, bright lights, the blare of the city. He'd gone into dives, prowled into every nook and hideaway in the maze of underworld Manhattan, but a dark house in the country needed a particular stoicism he'd never been called upon to develop.

He drew a deep breath, expanding his chest until it pressed against the outline of his shoulder holster. He ground the cigarette underheel, felt for his flashlight, then stepped across a flower bed and tried a French window experimentally. It was unfastened, and Devereaux pushed it open and moved silently into the house.

He played his flashlight, moving behind it with his ears alerted for sounds. He heard nothing and, soon oriented to the layout of the interior, he stopped behind a wide desk.

Devereaux had thumbed through a number of papers in practiced, professional search when the sound came. A rustling noise, like the wind, or the papers he was leafing through, echoing impossibly somewhere across the library. He shut off his flashlight, tensing, and then, aware that he was a silhouetted target against the great windows behind him, he dropped into a protective crouch behind the desk.

The noise came again, fainter this time, and Devereaux forced his mind and hearing, seeking to identify the sound and place its source. A long time passed, with the detective crouched restlessly, and in the continuing quiet he began to discount the alarm that had sent him to cover. He touched fingers to his gun, then withdrew them. He was a trespasser, there without warrant. He listened for another eternal minute, then stood up and played his flashlight across the room.

There were two blasts of flame in an almost simultaneous burst. His left arm went dead, and the top of his head began to burn. The last thing he was aware of before losing consciousness was the distorted cone of light on the rug where the flashlight lay, unhurt in its fall and still lighted.

2.

He came to feeling clean and sterile, as if he had been taken apart and reassembled, but with the weights of living abstracted. He watched the busy carnival of people around him idly, as if peering at the antics of a world distant to him, and which he viewed from a distance.

There were many men, some short and fat, some lean and tall, one watching him closely through thick glasses. There was a sheeted figure on the floor, and a girl with bare legs scribbling furiously into a notebook.

The eyes behind the thick glasses darted at him. "Feeling better?" the man asked.

Devereaux closed his eyes, then opened them, studying his interrogator intensely. He closed his eyes again to shut the man and the room out, then opened them, this time looking calmly from face to face. As the reality of the room settled upon him, the clean, sterile feeling departed and the weights were back inside him.

"How bad is it?" Devereaux asked moodily, struggling to a sitting position. He was on a divan.

"Messy wound in left hand. Bullet struck off, fortunately. I've given you a shot to prevent infection." The man behind thick glasses stuffed materials into a medical bag and pressed it closed. "Hand will take some time mending, and the sooner you get to a hospital and stay there the better," he continued pleasantly. "You're dosed up with painkiller now, but when it wears off—" He stopped, then pointed to Devereaux's head. "Nasty scalp wound up there. Painful but not serious." He made a small apologetic gesture. "We had to cut quite a bit of hair away."

"Who is everybody?" Devereaux said, fixing his gaze on the sheeted figure on the floor.

"Police," the doctor said, and moved away. A short, fat man took his place.

"Able to talk, Devereaux?" this man asked.

"Who's he?" Devereaux pointed at the sheeted figure.

"He's Frederick J. Castle. Was, I mean."

Devereaux stared incredulously, and the squat man continued, "Drilled through the back of the head. I'm Chief Bullard, Summit Police. We know who you are. We examined your wallet, made a telephone check. What we want is your story, the whole story." Bullard paused, then his face clouded. "Castle was an important man."

"Who'd he live here with?" Devereaux asked.

"A housekeeper, until a week ago. He let her go. Said he was going to close the house."

"Unmarried, was he?"

Bullard nodded, then said indignantly, "I'll ask the questions."

"Just two more," Devereaux smiled placatingly. "For the record, did you examine my gun?"

Bullard nodded. "It hadn't been fired." He added superfluously, "You didn't shoot Castle."

"Of course not. How long was I out?"

"Half hour. Maybe forty-five minutes."

"How'd you fellows know to come here?"

"A passing motorist heard a shot, and came scooting into town. Hey, that's three questions. Now tell me what you were doing here."

"First, who's she?" Devereaux asked, pointing at the girl with bare legs.

"Reporter on the town paper," Bullard replied irritably. "You're not answering my question."

Devereaux hesitated. Trespass, and across a state line, without warrant except his suspicions and a habit of thoroughness. Castle had a paramount right to shoot an intruder. An honest reply would trap him in a web of native attitudes, procedural knots, time-wasting nuisance and duress. He looked uneasily at Chief Bullard and his minions, and then at the dramatic absorption of the bare-legged scribe. The group promised complications. The Chief and his band were enjoying the release from suburban doldrums.

"I came on police business," Devereaux began evasively. "To ask Castle some questions pertaining to a case I'm interested in."

"What kind of case?" Bullard asked eagerly.

"Sorry, I'm not at liberty to say, at present."

"Castle was implicated?"

"Probably," Devereaux conceded meagerly. "Otherwise, why shoot me?"

"What happened between you? I mean, what happened to make him shoot you?"

"Nothing much happened, really. I'd, er, asked him if he knew a certain person in New York. When he denied it, I contradicted him, pointing out that he'd had a bite of supper recently with that certain person." Devereaux stopped, and watched the bare-legged girl scribbling industriously. "I guess there's something I've yet to find out about that made him desperate, because he suddenly pulled a gun on me and began shooting. I passed out, as you know." Devereaux paused. "That's about all."

Bullard was wrapped in thought. Soon he said disbelievingly, "He pulled a gun and began shooting? Just like that?"

Devereaux drew a long breath. "I forgot to say he said he was going to kill me, then claim I was an intruder he'd caught on his premises."

Bullard considered it. "Did Castle know you were coming?"

"Er, no. But he invited me in when I introduced myself."

"You haven't told us much," Bullard said disappointedly.

"There isn't much to tell. There'll be more when I break the case," Devereaux promised. He waited for an interval, watching the group do incidental things, then said, "Any reason why I can't be on my way?"

Waves of thoughts, hastily conceived and quickly discarded, passed over the Chief's homespun features. He was plainly racking his brain for a way of forcing himself into Devereaux's reticences.

"With things up in the air like this, I dunno," Bullard began lamely. "There's public opinion, Devereaux. Castle was a man of means. And then there's the inquest. We'll want you at the inquest."

"New York's just forty-five minutes away. I can get out here in a jiffy." Devereaux exhibited his bandaged hand. "I've got to get this attended to."

"We've got a mighty good hospital here in Summit," Bullard said hopefully.

Devereaux shook his head firmly. "I'll be better off in my own back yard."

Devereaux watched Bullard go to a library table. On it, piled over a spread newspaper, was a heaping of ash.

"Castle, or somebody, burned some papers in the fireplace," Bullard said to nobody in particular. He frowned at Devereaux helplessly. "We have the gun Castle used on you, but we haven't found the murder gun."

Devereaux kept his feeling of relief from showing in his face. Bullard lacked the tenacity it required to keep him in Summit. "I'll help all I can. We'll keep in close touch," Devereaux said. "Now, if you can spare a man to drive me back?"

"Wait," Bullard capitulated unhappily. "A Detective Solowey phoned he was on his way out here." He turned to his band suddenly and rasped, "Go through everything again. And comb the grounds, inch by inch. Find that murder gun."

3.

The Buick bumped over the Pulaski Skyway, gearing its speed to the caravan of cars ahead. They sat in silence, curiously untalkative, as if in flight from alien ground, as if even here, high up in the inky night and sealed in a moving automobile, there were hostile ears eavesdropping.

Devereaux's eyelids were drooping when Solowey's voice startled him. "Anders told me where you were. Bullard had phoned him. Anders is worried about what you're doing. Thinks my agency cover for you might not be legal enough. You better cancel those retirement papers or ask for temporary reinstatement or apply for a private license."

Devereaux said nothing, and Solowey looked over to him. "Hurt?" he asked compassionately.

"Arm's throbbing like crazy." The painkiller was wearing off.

"Castle wanted to kill you," Solowey said quietly. "That means something."

Devereaux said nothing, and Solowey continued, "That pile of ash. Castle built a bonfire of papers before getting shot."

"Or the killer did," Devereaux said.

"There might be a clue in that ash. If we could get it, and get it to a laboratory."

"Bullard won't let go, so forget it. We'll work with what we've got."

A mile later, Devereaux said, "It's finally become a murder case."

"It has," Solowey agreed solemnly, tooting the horn to pass a car ahead. "And you didn't have to go to Jersey to make it that."

It was slow filtering into Devereaux's consciousness. He realized it with a start. "Who?"

"Longo. Someone shot him on Front Street this afternoon."

"In broad daylight?" Devereaux asked incredulously.

"Best place to do it. Fish markets, boat whistles, trucks backfiring. A small-caliber bullet gets lost in the general uproar. Longo sat on a packing case near the wharf with a bullet hole in the side of the head near the ear. He was sitting for nearly an hour before anybody caught on that he was dead."

"He shook your man?"

"That was easy, once Longo knew he was being shadowed. There are office buildings downtown with three-way exits, and each exit leading to different streets."

Devereaux sighed wearily, "Damn, it's a day of surprises."

Solowey sounded a warning toot on the auto horn. "It is," he agreed. "It is," he repeated almost to himself.

"Drive to the Old New York Mission first, Solowey. You can drop me at Doc Freedley's after that."

"See Doc Freedley first," Solowey said, and Devereaux almost divined the rest by Solowey's tone. "Buloff's gone, bag and baggage. Disappeared. And that housekeeper of his, Anna Jorgensson, swore she didn't know his whereabouts." Solowey concluded wryly, "Sure, see Doc Freedley first."

Devereaux closed his eyes and began to doze off. There were electric needles racing from his hand to his shoulder, and a paste was forming on his forehead as his temperature rose. Sleep, he whispered to himself feverishly, was a blessed painkiller.

CHAPTER NINE

1.

Rain blew in a fine spray as if squeezed from a huge atomizer. It was dark for noontime, and the city glistened with a sweaty, oily film. Devereaux turned off the avenue briskly. The long tarpaulin coverall flapped with the action of his knees. His right arm was limp at his side, while the other swung along with his stride.

The Attic Circus sign was in wavering view when Devereaux crossed the street and descended a few cellar steps. His signal against the door went unanswered, and he was turning to leave when he saw the Venetian blind move. Peering eyes filled the freed space, and the wetness on the glass gave the illusion of eyes damp with tears.

The door opened, admitting Devereaux.

"You took your time," Pearl said sullenly.

"Just got your message this morning. Sorry." Devereaux indicated his limp arm. "I've been on the inactive list for the last forty-eight hours."

They faced each other in the center of the room for a silent moment, and Devereaux wondered about her strained look, the dead, unnatural whiteness of her skin that looked macabre under the fluorescent lights. She was without her customary rouge. Also without her customary aplomb. She looked tuckered out, depressed.

"Tell me about it," Devereaux said gently.

"Latimer tumbled to your idea. He tore up my concession contract the day after I sneaked that picture for you."

Devereaux's eyes glinted sympathetically. "I'll rustle up a new account for you."

Pearl shook her head. "I'm blackballed on this side of town. Latimer saw to that." She held up four fingers. "I've had this many cancellations since yesterday."

She went to the rear, motioning Devereaux to follow. "And I'm out of the picture-taking business," she said, kicking the plywood door open. "See for yourself."

Devereaux looked into the developing room. The modest equipment was a scattering of junk. A wrecker had come and gone. Devereaux picked a crushed camera off the floor and set it down on a long wooden table. "Latimer?" he asked tonelessly, feeling an anger even more than his wont.

She shook her head. "He wouldn't be fool enough. It was a guy I'd never seen around before." She cupped her cheeks with her hands. "My teeth ache," she said miserably. "I've been eating aspirins, but my teeth don't stop aching."

"He cuffed you?"

"His hands were like wooden paddles." Her fingers pressed into her cheeks. "Three days, and they keep on aching." Her voice cried, "No one ever hit me before, not ever. Not even my father."

She was trembling uncontrollably. Devereaux put an arm around her comfortingly, and she wept against his chest.

"This fellow," Devereaux said softly, "what did he look like?"

"A face you're afraid of. You see a lot of bad faces around, but you're not afraid of them. But this was a face you're afraid of."

"How will I know him, Pearl?"

She wiped her eyes on the handkerchief he held out to her. "You think he's only a kid, until you look close. Then you know he isn't a kid, because it takes more time than a kid's lived for a face to get that way." Devereaux felt her shudder. "His eyes aren't in his head. They're outside."

"Short, big, dark, what?" Devereaux prompted.

"You don't see that. You're just looking at his eyes."

A moment passed, and she crept closer to him. "Warm," she murmured. "So nice and warm."

"I'll find him," Devereaux promised grimly.

"It's good when it's so warm," she purred, snuggling. "My teeth feel good."

"How much to replace that equipment?"

"No, Johnny. I'll find a job."

Now the shelter was an embrace, and Devereaux felt a flush of embarrassment rise through him as her breathing became telltale. Her mouth changed form, and her body signaled him, but he was stone cold to her flesh.

It was too late for escape, and his compassion was too great. Devereaux met her mouth.

Funny thing, sex, he thought a while later. There was an excitement in him now, but not really for Pearl. Yet Pearl aroused it, and Pearl could satisfy it. Satisfy some of it, anyhow.

He held her at arm's length, found his handkerchief, and wiped a trickle of blood off his lip. "You kiss for keeps," he said smilingly.

"Take me somewhere, Johnny."

"Can't, not now. I've work."

"Then tonight. Take me out tonight. I want to laugh. Laugh and have fun." She pressed hard against him. "I've been in the dumps."

"Sounds like an idea," Devereaux said with artificial eagerness. "The minute I can I'll call you." He disengaged himself, and retreated to the door. "Right now I'm up to my neck."

He watched her eyes change as he smiled good-by. The change was easy to read. There was hurt, confusion, and also defeat. The date would never come off, and Pearl knew it. But in their embrace Devereaux had wanted her, and Pearl wisely knew that, too. And his rejection of her was a defeat that made her feel less of a woman.

Devereaux climbed the cellar steps remorsefully. He hadn't wanted to slight Pearl's womanliness. But what he needed was much more than Pearl, and he couldn't take less now.

He crossed the street. It was a dream, this thing he wanted, and it was growing late for dreaming. Of what consequence, he wondered, if a man and a woman, any pair, got into bed together? Why this damned, moralistic unnaturalness now, when he'd done exactly that through the whole of his life before?

He was looking at Sadye's portrait on the show poster of the Attic Circus when the truth suddenly dawned on him. He was in love with Jennifer Phillips.

2.

He sidestepped the headwaiter. A "Businessmen's Lunch: From $1.25" was being served, and the crowded tables attested the excellence of the restaurant's cuisine. The headwaiter frowned, then shrugged and turned away to his chores as Devereaux opened the private door that led through a short corridor to Latimer's inner sanctum.

He stopped, or was stopped, before a slightly built fellow who stood challengingly, as a guard stands, in front of Lippy's door.

Devereaux stared at the fellow, and recognition came almost immediately. The fellow was small, muscled like a dancer, with a shock of curly hair that fell forward to the brow. He was youthful looking, until you looked hard into his face. The face was Pearl's description come alive. Cold, with degenerate tracings, and curiously empty of expression. And the eyes, as Pearl had said, seemed outside the head.

Drugs, Devereaux decided. It was what eating drugs did to the eyes. The fellow was new to him, but a killer, surely.

He had seen too many through his twenty years to be mistaken. But high priced, this one. A costly import from somewhere. He had that air about him.

Devereaux stuck a hand out. "Let's have it," he ordered.

The fellow's eyes burned, and Devereaux reached and slapped him across the face. "Produce when a cop tells you to."

A crimson patch showed in the struck cheek, and as the fellow came away from his holster with his gun pointing at Devereaux, the door behind him opened and Lippy stood framed in it. He was wearing a beret and a green artist's smock.

"I'll take the gun," Devereaux said.

"You'll get it," the fellow said.

Latimer moved and got between them. "What's the idea, Devereaux?"

"I want his gun. And I want to see his permit to carry it."

"What damned right have you got? You're off the force."

"Don't you believe it, Lippy."

They eyed each other, and Lippy turned to the gunman. "Give it to him," he said, then turned back to Devereaux. "Permit is in my office. I got it for him myself."

Devereaux handled the surrendered gun. "Since when do you need an armed bodyguard, Lippy? Who are you afraid of?"

Lippy glared and said nothing.

"And where'd you import this reefer-eating hoodlum from?"

"You talk a lot, Devereaux."

Devereaux shouldered Lippy out of his path roughly and stared at the gunman. "Who are you, and where from?"

"Kansas City."

"I also asked your name."

"Artie Cabot."

"What's your record? How many murder raps did you beat in Kansas City?"

Cabot said nothing.

"How do you keep your hair so beautifully curled? Permanent wave, Artie, or homemade with a curling iron?"

Cabot reddened and said nothing.

"You don't like girls, do you?"

Cabot moved toward Devereaux threateningly.

"Try it, and I'll shoot you right in the guts, Artie. You like beating up girls, don't you? Bet you used to beat your mother and sister."

The bug eyes grew rounder and wilder, and Devereaux commanded, "Stick your hands out, palms up."

Cabot balled his hands into fists.

Latimer yelled fearfully, "What in hell are you getting at?"

"Shut up, Lippy." Devereaux repeated his command. "Your hands, Cabot. Palms up."

The gunman complied.

Devereaux studied the hands. "Strong, for a dainty little fellow. Not a minute's work on them, but hands like steel." There was a cold rage coursing through him. "Now face the wall, hands up high and palms on the wall."

The gunman complied, and a look of distress came over Lippy's face. "Devereaux, you've gone crazy!"

"Shut up, Lippy." Devereaux moved closer to the gunman. "Press your palms against the wall. Hard!"

Distress changed rapidly to horror in Lippy's face as Devereaux turned the gun in his hand, clasped the barrel firmly, then brought the butt end down on one of the gunman's hands with shattering force.

The hand dropped uselessly, and the gunman wheeled with anguish burned into his features. "As you were," Devereaux said savagely. "Both hands in a cast, and you're getting off cheap. Turn and take it without whimpering."

The underlip stopped trembling, and the face seemed to grow curiously calm and indifferent in a remarkable example of will power. The gunman turned and put both hands

82

firmly on the wall. The broken hand was just a trifle lower than its mate.

Devereaux brought the butt end of the gun down. There was a cracking noise, and specks of painted plaster blew with the concussion.

There was no outcry. Cabot remained motionless, mute with shock, with his hands up and his head tipped forward, as if impaled on the wall.

"There's a night train back to Kansas City," Devereaux said tonelessly.

A little while later, Devereaux said, "Whenever you get on the phone about this, Lippy, think of Pearl." His eyes held Lippy implacably. "You owe her about five hundred dollars for equipment."

Lippy nodded mechanically.

Devereaux said, "Thirty teeth in her mouth, more or less. And a toothache in every one of them." He handed the gun to Lippy. "I'm a tough cop, I suppose," he continued quietly, watching Cabot's hands slide slowly down the walls like giant ugly insects. "No heart, and sadistic, the way cops sometimes get after a lifetime of dealings with riffraff and killers." Devereaux paused. Why, he wondered, was he now defending his act. He suddenly thought of Solowey. Solowey wouldn't approve of his maiming of Cabot, even Cabot.

"Cabot hurt the girl, and two wrongs don't make a right, I know," Devereaux resumed restlessly, staring at the discolored hands dangling lifelessly at the gunman's sides. "But Pearl will be glad to know someone championed her, even if a little late. She's entitled to five minutes' worth of male protection, Lippy, because her father was an honest man and Pearl remembers him."

Lippy had the look of a man listening perforce to a lunatic. Devereaux looked at him, then away from him. Finally he shrugged. The point he was laboring was unclear even to himself.

"Let's go inside and get down to cases," Devereaux said.

"You're crazy," Lippy said disgustedly, "a crazy bastard." He followed Devereaux into his office.

3.

The overstuffed chairs were deep and roomy, and the wall hangings mirrored the American sports world. There were pictures of Man o' War and Seabiscuit, Dempsey and Firpo opposing each other in a prize ring, John J. McGraw in a New York Giants uniform, and a picture of Lippy Latimer accepting the award of a diamond belt. The large painter's easel against a wall was an odd and anomalous note.

Lippy turned away from Devereaux, and began to apply paint to a canvas in process as if oblivious to the detective.

Devereaux studied the canvas, watching Lippy's rapid method with a palette knife. The scene was the back yard of a slum dwelling. It held clotheslines of colored wash, an overturned ashcan with scavenging cats busy in the debris, patches of grass that formed little scattered islands in the broken cement. It was inexpert, crude, primitive, but the colors were bold and it had a curious force.

"You paint like you fought, Lippy."

"Then I'm a champ."

The side of Lippy's face that was partly paralyzed was in Devereaux's view. It was odd hearing speech while watching a cheek that was virtually dead to movement. Devereaux moved to the other side of Latimer.

"Get a bang out of it, huh?" the detective said.

Lippy said nothing, and placed sun highlights on the ashcan with the mechanical sureness of a building plasterer.

"What started you painting?"

"Quit buttering me."

"I'm interested."

"Crap."

"For a fact, Lippy."

"Doctor's idea," said Lippy, relenting. "I paint to forget I've got half a face. Okay?" Lippy applied a thick flame-red

84

to B.V.D.'s hanging on a clothesline. "Now get down to it, or scram."

"Can't talk to your back."

"To my rear end."

Devereaux suppressed an emotion, and stuck his hands in his pockets. "Tell me about Martin Phillips."

"He eats in my joint."

"Nothing else?"

"Period. He eats in my joint, period."

"Then tell me about Frederick J. Castle."

"He's a friend of Phillips."

"Was."

"You don't say." Lippy outlined a fence in the foreground by drawing a line with the edge of his palette knife.

"It's been in the papers."

"I only read *Li'l Abner.*"

"No special interest in Castle?"

Lippy shook his head and kept on painting.

"How about Pearl?"

"Cabot's own idea. You said he didn't like girls."

"You tore up her concession contract."

"She had it coming."

"For photographing Castle?"

"Without being asked."

"But why should you care?"

Lippy drew in boards on the fence. "My customers are entitled to any privacy they want."

"I still ask, why should you care?"

"Castle asked me to get the negative."

Devereaux regarded Lippy's profile solemnly. "How did he know there was a negative?"

"The broad was as smooth as a burglar with a bell up his behind. She faked taking a picture of the table next to Castle's. When an hour passed and there was no delivery of the picture, Castle got suspicious."

"Turn around and talk, Lippy."

"I still like you talking to my rear end better."

"Afraid I'll read your face?"

"Why don't you scram now?"

Devereaux held himself rigid. "You went to bat for Castle big."

"Pearl had no business stooging for you. Not in my joint."

"Didn't you wonder why Castle was so camera shy?"

"I don't give a damn why. The little bitch had no business taking a picture without the customer's authorization."

Devereaux lit a cigarette and watched Lippy mix a muddy gray color on his palette. He paced the room thoughtfully, scanned a row of books set between big onyx bookends on Lippy's desk, then selected one. It was a thick paper-covered book titled *The Book of Champions*.

Devereaux read the alphabetical index in the back, and found "Latimer." He was aware of Lippy's brief, backward glance as he turned to page 113 and lingered over the opening lines of Lippy's ring history.

LATIMER, THOMAS (LIPPY): Born San Francisco, Cal., March 15, 1905. Middleweight, World Champion, 1929, 30, 31. Lifetime record: Won 26, Lost 2. No Decision, 4. K.O. 18. K.O. by 1.

The data below were a chronological listing of the date, place, opponent, and the outcome of Lippy's thirty-two ring battles.

Devereaux read through it, then referred to comparative biographic accounts of other fighters. Soon he placed the book face down on the desk and inquired casually, "Ever go to school, Lippy?"

Lippy put his paint materials down and turned to Devereaux. "That meant to be a crack?"

"Sketch of your career just says you were born."

"What about it?"

86

"And your father and mother," Devereaux continued mildly. "No plug for them, no mention."

"So?"

"Take this sketch right ahead of yours." Devereaux picked the book up and read:

HERMAN, VINCENT (KID): Born Butte, Mont., Sept. 16, 1902. To Emil Herman and Sarah Curtis. Schools, St. Mary Parochial, Seattle Business College. Middleweight Contender, 1923-28. Lifetime Record: Won 44. Lost 10. No Decision 2. K.O. 16. K.O. by 5.

Devereaux looked up. "See what I mean?"

"You talk like a goddam press agent."

"Like a detective."

"Will you scram the hell outa here!" Lippy shouted.

"Question too tough for you?" Devereaux persisted.

Lippy stared. "Is this a joke?"

"No."

"You want the story of my life?" The bewilderment in Lippy's face seemed genuine.

"In effect, yes. Where you came from, what schools, who are your people?"

"Why don't you go to the newspapers? They got enough on me to keep you reading for a year."

"Later. But I want your version first."

"And if I throw you outa here on your ear?"

Devereaux's expression hardened. "Then I'll make arrangements to sweat you downtown."

"And this has to do with what?"

"Murder. Castle and an ex-con named Longo."

"Now, who the hell's Longo?"

"Some other time. First, your story."

"Dammit." Lippy glowered balefully while his mobile cheek worked fitfully. "You must be smelling the stuff!" He clenched and unclenched his fists. "You break a guy's hands out there, then come in here to get my goat. Why I gotta take abuse from a hopped-up, crazy sonofabitch!"

"Your story, Lippy."

"Okay," Lippy finally said, recovering control. "Your round." His jaw jutted forward. "But you'll hate yourself for picking a fight with me."

"Talk, Lippy."

"Frisco. Like the book says, I was born in Frisco. The date's a phony. It's a phony because I don't know my real birthdate. I never saw my birth certificate. No one ever showed me one. I was an orphan almost from the word go."

"Who brought you up?"

"I brought myself up. There was a rummy named Cameron I used to rush the growler for when I was five. I called him uncle, until he skipped out one day. Then there was a skinny old lady I called Mrs. Teague. I was in a big parade behind a hearse when I was ten." Lippy grinned humorlessly. "Mrs. Teague was in the hearse. A big broad sitting next to me kept slapping my face because I wasn't crying. After that, I worked for a maniac named Schmidt who ran a saloon and hated kids. I remember sweeping up, peeling spuds in a stinking kitchen, scrubbing kitchen pots that made me throw up, and sleeping on a hard floor. I skipped off when I was thirteen. Began to ship from Frisco to Honolulu and back as cabin boy on those big liners. Next thing I knew I was eighteen, racking 'em up in a Seattle poolroom, and living with a doll twice my age in a three-dollar-a-week flop." Lippy paused, then said gloomily, "Now, for chrissakes, will you scram."

"What schools did you attend?"

Lippy puckered his brow. "Public school whatchmacallit. To remember the number I'd have to be Einstein. There was a teacher who kept sending me home to wash up and get the lice outa my hair. There was a teacher who sent me home because my ass was showing through a hole in my pants. There was a teacher who claimed I swiped the Ingersoll watch she kept on her desk. There was a truant officer who beaned me with a milk bottle when I beat him over a fence." Lippy shrugged. "What I remember most is concentrating on how to steal the other kids' lunch." He looked hard at Devereaux. "Okay, I told you."

"How'd you break into the fight game?"

"That Seattle poolroom job I got when I was eighteen. Big hangout, with a dice room, gym, and a prize ring in the rear. Pugs used to work out there, give ambitious kids pointers. I picked up enough technique to come East and buck for a club booking."

"Right away?"

Lippy shook his head. "Didn't get a chance to box pro for four years. Drove a truck, stevedored, while waiting for my chance. Finally got my start in the amateurs. The Golden Gloves." Lippy concluded irritably, "The rest you know, unless you're deaf, dumb, and blind."

Devereaux nodded. The rest of Latimer's story was history. A meteoric rise from preliminary boy to ranking contender, and finally world's champion. Latimer's unorthodox style and famed shock punch, and the managerial wizardry of Zach Spiro, were star chapters in pugilism's story book.

The detective looked at Latimer curiously. Remembered pain, buried but not erased with time, was etched in the ex-pugilist's homespun face. Lippy looked orphaned, lost, as if by looking behind him he had been stripped of his successes.

"Dammit," Lippy said morosely, "I feel like getting plastered."

"Sorry," Devereaux said, aware that Lippy's fanatical sobriety was a classic Broadway vignette.

"Aw, crap." Lippy seemed to heave with the epithet, as if tearing himself from his own past in one mighty spasm. "You got what you wanted," he said harshly. "Now whaddaya hanging around for!"

What he wanted? Devereaux picked at Lippy's tale thoughtfully. Item, item, item, blank, blank, blank, a great nebulous void. A world's middleweight champion has leaped from a gigantic, uncharted, undated, nameless emptiness into a nation's consciousness.

"I didn't get a thing from your story," Devereaux said.

Lippy scowled and said nothing.

"Not a thing," Devereaux repeated, with his eyes intent on Lippy's face. "Nothing that acquits you in my suspisions."

"You're talking riddles."

"I can't pin you anywhere to your past before you came to public notice as a fighter."

After a hostile pause, Devereaux said quietly, "Bet people and places you knew as a kid went up in smoke long ago. Bet that poolroom in Seattle doesn't exist any more."

Lippy nodded. "The building was torn down. There's a public playground there now." The ex-pugilist's face darkened. "What're you driving at?"

"An amazing coincidence. Castle, Phillips, and now you."

"What about us?"

"No early background I can pin any of you to." Devereaux smiled faintly. "It gets frustrating for a detective. Starts him imagining things."

"Imagining what?" Latimer demanded wrathfully.

"That maybe three men lack a past because there's something hidden in that past. Some skeleton they each hold a claim check to."

"You're nuts."

"Maybe," Devereaux agreed. "Maybe my imagination is running away. But you were three men in a huddle a few nights ago. And you *did* go to bat for Castle way beyond the call of duty." The detective's voice sharpened. "A mysteriously murdered publisher, a swishing critic who scares when a detective visits him, and an ex-pug who imports a killer for protection. Kind of a weird trio, Lippy."

"You oughta quit smelling the stuff," Lippy said.

"Why'd you import a bodyguard?"

"I been stuck up for my receipts twice this season. Insurance company threatened to cancel my policy. You can check those stick-ups with headquarters, wise guy."

Devereaux sought Lippy's eyes unsuccessfully. The ex-pugilist turned away, went back to his easel, and began studying his handiwork.

"Who are you afraid of, Lippy?"

"I been stuck up twice, I told you."

"You didn't hire a guard. You imported a killer."

"Go to hell."

Devereaux shrugged and went to the door. "You came up the hard way, Latimer, and I respect you for it." A shadow crossed the detective's face. "I slugged my way to respectability from a Chicago tenement myself. You had an uncle who disappeared; I had an aunt who died of tuberculosis when I was nine."

Lippy turned slowly, as if drawn by the unwonted softness in Devereaux's tone, and stared at the detective. Devereaux continued earnestly, "I hate crooks. Maybe because I fought like a wildcat against becoming one all the time I starved as a kid. Catch a crook, and nine times out of ten he's been robbing the fellow born right next door in the same tenement as himself." Devereaux paused. "You know my record, and you know that I don't make propositions. But if my guess about you is right, I'm asking you to come out from under. Line up on my side."

Lippy shook his head vaguely. His eyes were now elsewhere, and he seemed preoccupied with something far away and remote. Devereaux said, "I'll help you, befriend you as far as the law allows."

Lippy said huskily, "Stop, you'll make me bust out crying."

"I'd hate to see you get hurt."

"You're crazy with hop."

"I'd hate to see you get killed."

Lippy's eyes bulged, and he seemed to quiver. Finally he said in a weary, automatic sort of way, "Beat it. Go peddle your hop somewhere else."

CHAPTER TEN

1.

The broken piano arrangements were subtle pushes feeling out his defenses. Devereaux's eyes were casual as he watched her balancing on one leg with her middle hollowed out, yet standing with reedlike rigidity, as if a string were running from the top of her head to the floor.

Soon the sudden stretches and acrobatics were over, and the dance mood changed. The piano stopped, and a finger drum started up an African piece. The dancers began sensual, undulating movements.

His eyes fixed on her, deep in the group, but moving in a graceful solo designed only for him. She was brilliantly white in her black leotard. As the tempo grew, the tom-toms beating from the finger drum pierced his defenses. His eyes warmed until they were swimming in a haze.

Not long after, she came out of a dressing room, and crossed the barren loft floor to Devereaux's bench. The detective climbed up on his feet precariously. Something had gone wrong with his machinery.

"I promised myself once that I'd watch you dance," he said.

"Was it all too incomprehensible?" She smiled.

"Over my head, the modern ballet," Devereaux confessed. "Got a bang out of it, though." He took her arm. "You'll have to explain it to me sometime. I was raised on a simple diet of Radio City Rockettes and Pat Rooney, Senior."

On the street, he plunged into his pockets absently, and left a reckless showering of coins in a panhandler's hand.

They turned off Fifty-ninth Street. Abreast of his Buick, Devereaux motioned to a large illuminated sign that announced: HAMBURGER HEAVEN.

She shook her head. "Not hungry enough, thanks. And I daren't eat between meals."

"Then get in. We'll park somewhere and talk."

A half hour had passed, and Devereaux talked like a man in a rush to spend a burden that was perversely accumulating as he spoke and probed. He had the odd feeling that talk of murder and conspiracy was an irrelevant and wasteful business here with the harbor stretching before them.

"That's about all there is," the detective said finally. "It's a murder case, and a complicated one."

"Is—he involved?"

"Phillips?" Devereaux nodded gravely.

A gong clanged somewhere on the river, and a tugboat with water spouting from a round hole in its bottom chugged by. Her eyes followed its course until her head completed a half-circle and she was looking at Devereaux's profile. He twisted slightly to meet her eyes.

"He's been a wild man," she said. "And I can see why he would be, now."

"Anything new? In his attitude toward you, I mean."

Her shiver coursed through him. "He's surly. I catch him staring at me as if—" She stopped with her face knotting, her thoughts pushing.

"As if?" Devereaux prompted.

"As if I were a hated intruder. As if he were trying to glare me away."

"As if he'd begun to repent that purchase," Devereaux said.

She nodded and looked earnestly into the detective's face. "What's my part in all you've told me?"

"You're just an odd cutout in a jigsaw, so far. Where you place, I don't know." Devereaux smiled faintly. "I got more than I bargained for when I took you on that first evening."

She seemed to move closer, in an instinctive huddling. A leg found his, stayed, touching near the knee, as if wordlessly telling of her regret, begging his patience.

"I'm in for the whole ride," Devereaux said. "Even if you were fat and forty or didn't exist, I'd stay to the finish. Events have decided that for me."

"Lippy Latimer," she said, as if turning the name in her mind. "What does he look like?"

"Heavy set, beefy in the face. Sportily dressed. Wears colored silk neckties. Left side of his face is partly paralyzed. Talking comes hard."

Her head was nodding with his description.

"You've seen him?"

"Yes. He visited. There was unpleasantness, words."

"Hear what was said?"

"No. I just caught a glimpse of him when he came in, and again later when he left."

"They're all in it, whatever it is, up to their teeth," Devereaux said grimly. "And there's mistrust, no love lost anywhere. There's a killer loose somewhere, and whatever it is that binds them together must be bigger than life, and bigger than death."

Her face brooded for a moment, then fixed on Devereaux with a look of implicit belief and faith.

"No bouquets, please," Devereaux said. He laughed shortly. "The fact is, I know zero subtracted from nothing. I haven't the slightest notion of where to go from here. Any next move I make is strictly out of confusion."

A silence fell, and Devereaux settled back in his seat, contentedly aware of her nearness. And soon, when the last echo of talk had died, he crooked his arm and she crept into its shelter. She rubbed her cheek against his shoulder, and he bent to kiss her on the mouth.

She met his lips eagerly, and murder and pursuit were suddenly light-years away.

A gong sounded somewhere on the river, and they parted as if responding to a signal. They sat up, watching the life on the river.

"You're different," she said, and her eyes were sparkling.

"Different than what?"

"Different than before." She sighed. "I thought you'd never kiss me again."

Devereaux smiled a wan smile. "Had to, finally, I guess. The struggle was too uneven. A man begins with a handicap."

"Handicap?"

"His being a man."

"Oh," she said, with the wisdom of thousands of years of mothers of men.

2.

The official was a fat man with a fleshy face that looked mauled. He had the sedentary air of a man who had spent his best years in the narrow corner behind a desk.

The official brushed Devereaux's proffered credentials aside with a reproachful look. "Your face is almost as familiar to me as my own," he said, and motioned the detective to a chair. He lumbered to a nest of wall buttons, and the dimly lit gloom changed to a bleak, overlighted whiteness.

"Coffee?" the official asked affably.

Devereaux nodded gratefully, and the official poured a carefully measured half from a container. He pushed a glass toward the detective, and tilted the container to his mouth.

There was a small, compatible exchange, and Devereaux launched into the purpose of his late evening drive to Ossining, New York.

Soon the general outline of Devereaux's story was told, and the official looked mystified. His indefinite chin fell deeper into layers of neck flesh, and the corners of his mouth drew into rutted lines of deprecation.

"Sounds to me like a long ride for very little. Why didn't you just telephone?"

"I like everything firsthand and personal. Even failure."

The official smiled, as if to show that the wisdom latent in Devereaux's remark was not lost to him. "There's your genius, right in that statement," he said, then resumed looking mystified. "But I still can't see anything in our files here on Longo worth a minute of your time. He served time until his parole, and that's all." He looked at Devereaux's face, then flicked a button of the inter-communications system.

"I'll get the file anyhow, and you can satisfy yourself," the official said.

Devereaux waited through the official's instructions to the Sing Sing record room. "My idea is that Longo wanted to be arrested, convicted, and sent up. The way it happened has me convinced he asked for it."

"That's a pretty big idea."

"The case is like that. Big. Big enough for a couple of murders."

The chin came forward out of its groove. "Maybe Longo asked to be arrested, as you say, but for a more likely reason. Not because he wanted to do time here, but just to be taken out of circulation.

"He was hot," the official continued. "Somebody was out to give him his lumps. Lots of crooks hide out in jail." He smiled. "Where else can you get lodging and armed body-guards without a cent cost?"

Devereaux nodded. It was a possibility, and he'd thought of it, too. But reluctantly, because it stifled imagination by drawing a blind on a promising view.

"It's the more obvious answer perhaps, but I won't buy it for now," Devereaux said. "The way Longo was sprung, and the character of his sponsor, Buloff, suggest a lot more than a penny-ante dip looking to Sing Sing for temporary cover from some personal danger. There was a deep game going on, with quite important people mixed up in it, and Longo was an important pawn."

An aide entered unobtrusively, deposited a file on the official's desk, and left without a word. The official opened the folder, fingered through its contents, and shrugged his shoulders.

"There it is. A routine story. Longo did time, and that's all." He slid the file across the desk to Devereaux.

Devereaux went through it, absorbed in each page, then turning to another methodically. It was a drab, mechanically impersonal, chart bulletin of one Nick Longo, Convict No. 116271, duly received at Sing Sing on a given day in accordance with a sentence meted out by a Judge Bamberger, housed in Cell Block C-4 for a prescribed length of time, and finally paroled sixteen months before the expiration of his term sentence.

Devereaux sighed heavily. As the official had argued, the findings were worth exactly five minutes on the telephone. The night ride had been a gratuitous and whimsical act.

The detective looked up. "It says that Number 116271 dined, slept, and sunned himself in the prison yard at taxpayers' expense for a period of time." He grimaced. "About as illuminating as a burned-out electric bulb." His brow corded, and his eyes fixed speculatively on the official. "Ignoring the mechanical facts, what was the human story of Longo's stay here? F'rinstance, who did he bunk with? Who were his cronies here? Who did he seek out to chum with?"

Devereaux added as a pointed afterthought, "And who did he war with?"

The official lifted a shoulder. "McGuire can answer that. He's head guard over in C-4."

"Get McGuire."

The official looked dubious. "Don't want to be a wet

towel, but is it worth it? McGuire's long on memory, but a regiment of prisoners come and go, and it's been a long time since Longo."

Devereaux made a face. "Maybe it's not worth it. And the chances are it is a waste of time. But show me a thorough investigator, and I'll show you a timewaster. A timewaster because he's thorough."

"You've made your point." The official smiled. "I'll ring for McGuire."

Five minutes passed, and a spare man with a deep pallor came in.

Devereaux smiled his acknowledgment on being introduced. "The Warden says you're long on memory, McGuire," the detective said.

First McGuire nodded cautiously, then threw conservatism to the winds. "They once pinned a medal on my memory." He grinned proudly. "I picked a killer right off a public sidewalk. The case was a dozen years old, written off the books as unsolved, and my man had had a fancy face-lifting job done on him."

Devereaux smiled in perfunctory approval. "Remember Nick Longo?" he asked.

McGuire looked baffled. "Longo?" he repeated emptily in a crestfallen tone.

"He served time in your section. Number 116271."

McGuire's face lighted, and his head went up and down. "Mousy little fellow. In on a Sullivan Law conviction."

Devereaux said eagerly, "Remember him as clearly as that?"

McGuire savored his moment. "Sure do," he said, wearing figurative thumbs in his vest.

"What were your impressions of Longo?"

"Nothing special. Just another fellow serving time."

"Troublemaker?"

"No. Short termers never are." The guard paused, and his eyes looked vacant, as if sight was turned inward, on the past. "Matter of fact," he resumed after a few moments, "Longo was so easy to handle we put him to use."

"How?"

"Odd jobs. Inventory clerk in the work rooms. Messenger work in the library."

"As a trusty?"

"Sort of, but not officially. He was too much of a short termer for that." The guard's head arched inquiringly. "If you'd give me an idea of what you're after—"

"I'm working on the theory that Longo wanted to be sent up the river. That he deliberately maneuvered his way into Sing Sing."

The guard looked incredulous, and Devereaux overleaped explanations impatiently. "Did Longo chum with anybody here? Who were his cronies?"

The answer came slowly. "Nobody specially, as far as I know. But I can check, ask around," he volunteered.

Devereaux nodded. "You may have to. I'll want to know who Longo was friendly with, and whom he was antagonistic toward." The detective continued with slow emphasis. "Especially the latter. I'm particularly interested in knowing toward whom Longo showed dislike and hostility."

"That's a tall order at this late date," the guard said doubtfully. "Anyhow, I said Longo was no troublemaker."

"No sudden distemper or petty argument, ever? No stir nerves? No cliquing, this pair against that pair? No ragging another prisoner, even if just out of boredom? No complaints against him, even petty ones? No disciplinary counts against him, even trifling ones?"

The guard shook his head. "I don't remember any. But I can check."

"Sure, do that." Devereaux ran teeth over his lower lip contemplatively. "Meanwhile, still off the top of your head. Were there any incidents during Longo's time here?"

"Incidents?" The guard was puzzled.

"Something Longo might have been implicated in, but

behind the scenes. Some outbreak. A row, maybe. Violence in the laundry or yard or dining hall." The detective's tones quickened as the idea took hold. "A garroting, stabbing, an assault. Someone was rushed to emergency, maybe. Someone cashed in."

The guard turned a palm up apologetically. "You got my memory doing somersaults. Off the top of my head, the answer is no, nothing. But I'd rather report from the records."

Devereaux nodded understandingly, and McGuire hurried out of the room.

The detective's eyelids were drooping when McGuire returned. He was carrying two large thick books, like ledgers. The date by year was lettered across them.

"Nothing," the guard said, shaking his head. "I went through the section record, page by page, day by day, for the period Longo served. No outbreak, no assault, no nothing. The record's clean."

Devereaux leafed through the ledger pages mechanically, his mind busily turning ideas and discarding them as quickly. He was conscious of a steady thinning of purpose and a growing dispiritedness. His theory about Longo was wasting for substance.

"I'll need an orientation course on how to decipher all this stuff," the detective grinned weakly. His eyes were blurring.

"As I said, there's nothing to read. Nothing of what you're after." The guard rubbed his chin doubtfully. "I can ask around in the morning. Maybe learn something about Longo from the inmates."

Devereaux voiced a discarded idea. "When nosing around, keep in mind that Longo might have planted himself in Sing Sing to get close to somebody. Chum with that somebody, and pump him. A stoolie dodge, with the idea of double-cross behind it."

The guard nodded dutifully, and Devereaux returned his gaze to the books. The ledgers were a carefully detailed greengrocer's account of every great and small activity in the prison section. The drab routine of days without end, the dreary log of men in cages, stultified by monotony and sameness, were noted in handscript. Devereaux plodded patiently through the mass of entries that recalled men amortizing a group debit of thousands of years, men being fed, diverted, disciplined, assigned to shop or some occupational therapy, evaluated, tested for aptitudes, treated for cuts in the machine shop, restricted, privileged, rushed to surgery with bursting appendixes, injured.

Devereaux looked up thoughtfully. "Deaths. Convicts die, too, and I've skimmed past a gang of them already," he said loosely, letting the seed of a sudden idea fertilize in his thinking.

The guard smiled. "We got a select old men's club here. Only over sixty's are eligible. The mortality rate is high."

"Besides hearts giving," Devereaux interrupted impatiently. "Forgetting normal deaths. Was there a death of unusual character? Someone slipped and cracked his skull. Someone tangled with shop machinery. Was there something like that, something accidental?"

The guard nodded. "One accidental death. Frankie Hughes."

"What kind of an accident was it?"

McGuire looked distressed for the memory. "A freak accident, and pretty terrible. Scalded to death. He fainted while showering." His tone deprecated Devereaux's look of avid interest. "Strictly an accident. We're clear on that. We checked carefully. Frankie Hughes was a victim of chronic dizzy spells."

"How come the water ran that hot?"

The guard smiled. "We thought of that angle. Bad plumbing. Sometimes one line or the other, the hot tap or the cold, peters out. You're under the shower when suddenly you jump."

"Not even an outside chance of foul play?"

The guard shook his head firmly. "It wasn't the first faint Frankie Hughes pulled, even if it was the last. Also, Hughes was popular with everybody, unpopular with nobody." A reminiscent smile played around the guard's eyes. "A real gentleman, Hughes. Always reading books. Crazy about books. The guards liked him; the prisoners liked him. We called him Professor."

"Anybody see it happen?"

"Not right away. Hughes was alone in the shower room. The whole thing took less than ten minutes."

"What was Hughes in for?"

"Armed robbery and a shooting. He was doing sixty years. He'd already done twenty. That's all I can tell you about him, except that he was no more than a kid when he was sent up. He was hardly past forty when he cashed in."

Devereaux found a pad and pencil and made some notes. The guard looked at the detective critically. "Don't bite too hard on it," he admonished.

Outside, Devereaux gulped deep draughts of air. The night was cold. There was some wind, and the clouds filing across the moon promised storm. He stamped down a bristling troop of thoughts. Time enough another day, he told himself. His brain would sleep, and a mechanical man would zoom the Buick New Yorkward. He hurried across the lawn toward the gates with the grass whipping at his trouser cuffs. The Buick was a long walk away, outside the prison grounds.

3.

The speedometer climbed to fifty, fifty-five, spurted to sixty-five, then leveled off at sixty. Towering mountain rock flanked one side of the narrow river roadway like a canyon wall. On the other side, a sharp declivity plunged toward the river.

Devereaux's foot touched the brake lightly as he maneuvered the car into the abrupt and treacherous circle of a hairpin curve.

His headlights were darting patterns moving along the bluffs, and the road was suddenly lost. His hands worked the wheel excitedly while the instantaneous apprehension that the mechanical man had somehow lost control of the machine flashed through him. His foot played the brake, and he was conscious of a new and unfamiliar element that made the Buick strange to his reflexes.

A hand flicked the ignition key off as the Buick angled helplessly into a corner of the bluff, then seemed to fold against it like an accordion telescoping. Devereaux's head jerked forward and down, as if dealt a rabbit punch by an invisible puncher.

He was alive, conscious, bent over the wheel like a man snatching forty winks, with the mountain rock before him hanging from the sky like a stone curtain.

He had an idiotic urge to laugh, let himself go in gales of laughter.

CHAPTER ELEVEN

1.

Devereaux leaned into the forward booth and nudged the cabdriver. "Make a right, and then turn left. See if the blue sedan a hundred yards back stays on our tail."

There was an uncertain dissenting mumble, and Devereaux thrust a hand into the driver's booth. His palm opened to show police credentials.

"Wanna shake him?" the cabdriver said eagerly, leaping into a whole alliance with the drama.

"No. I just want to confirm the fact that he's tailing us."

"Who is the joker?" The cabdriver sought to widen the area of confidence.

Devereaux made a gesture behind him. "The sun's at our back, and I can't see."

The cab turned right at the corner, covered a block, and turned left.

The sun was still behind them in a blinding haze. Devereaux held his hand to his brow as a visor, and peered into the haze.

The blue sedan was about a hundred yards back.

A mile farther the cabdriver asked, "Drop you any special place?"

"Right abreast of that parked Buick." The detective pointed.

Devereaux surveyed the Buick ruefully as the cab parked double with it. Its flashing luster had dimmed. Its newness was gone; it looked secondhand. The front-end repair had been rushed, but literally. The sleek, polished front fenders and hood were pockmarked.

The emergency driver from upstate approached the unhappy detective and dropped his mite into the gloom.

"Hammered her back into shape as good as we could. We worked on it all night. Looks a little beat up on the outside, but she's mechanically okay."

Devereaux fretted through his wallet moodily, searching for a suitable tip.

2.

When the tale was done, Solowey's eyes glinted sympathetically and his face brooded in complete identification with Devereaux's moments of near-disaster.

"The miracle was," Devereaux said, "that I didn't go crashing down into the river. The right front wheel fell off first, and that's what saved me. I eased into the bluffs with a stiff neck and a sore jaw where the wheel met my chin."

"All four wheels were loosened, hmm," Solowey said superfluously.

"And the few nuts left securing the wheels were all on the last thread of the bolts on the drum. The idea was specially tailored for those curves on the Ossining approaches." Devereaux grinned humorlessly. "A smart stunt."

"It was done up there, in Ossining," Solowey said. "You were trailed driving up."

Devereaux nodded and went to the window. "I go nowhere unescorted now." Solowey joined him at the window curiously, and Devereaux pointed into the street.

"That blue sedan parallel with the White Rose Bar."

"Who?" Solowey frowned.

"Buloff."

Solowey stared into space as if reading some secret writing. "The probability is," he said after a moment, "that Buloff made that trip with you to Ossining."

Devereaux nodded darkly. "I'll buy that."

"This concentration on you has the promise of climax."

"Sudden death, huh? Mine."

Solowey matched his colleague's grin. "Or a break in the case. You are marked for death, and that must mean that you are close to an important discovery."

Devereaux made a face. "Let's not bow to our own applause, huh? Let's have the research."

Solowey pulled a drawer open, then waved a sheet of paper. "I'm spending a retired detective's life savings with the fine disregard of a gold digger." He read from the sheet and clucked his tongue. "A new four-hundred-dollar total. The operative who looked into Latimer's background put two lobster dinners and a plane ride to California on his expense account. Two lobster dinners in one day!"

"Was he worth it?"

Solowey's face drew doubtfully. "Just as you predicted. Nothing Latimer told you could be proved or disproved. One possible break in Latimer's story developed, however." The stout man's tone deprecated the finding. "A sports writer on a San Francisco newspaper, a regular old-timer, was ready to swear that Lippy Latimer was originally a Brooklyn boy."

"On what did he base his belief?"

"An amateur tournament in the middle twenties. He said he had watched an evening of boxing events in a prize ring in the rear gymnasium-clubroom quarters of an East New York, Brooklyn poolroom. The sports writer was there as a guest of the referee. He said Lippy was the semi-finalist, fighting under the name of Kid Young."

Devereaux frowned. "An amateur bout of that kind is seldom a matter of official record. And Latimer was a baby in the middle twenties." A pause later he added, "What was the name of the pool hall?"

"Marco's Recreation Parlor and Athletic Club." The corners of Solowey's mouth turned up in a faint smile. "There's a housing development on the site now. I already checked." He shook his head. "It means something, maybe, but we have nothing more than an ancient memory of an aged sports writer to go by. It is scarcely worth your confronting Latimer with it, my friend."

"I'll spring it on him, anyhow, with a few trumped-up garnishments to give it a little more weight, make the contradiction in his story about his past more glaring." Devereaux shrugged. "It might build to something. Who knows? Latimer's pretty unnerved as it is, close to jitters, if that imported bodyguard means what it suggests. A nudge might start him talking, really talking. A push might start him screaming." He exchanged a smile with Solowey. "What about Buloff?"

Solowey beamed. "There we got a bargain. Our second operative feasted on peanut-butter sandwiches and traveled by subway."

"But what did he get?"

"A pedigree, finally, and not a blank page. A pedigree more than a yard long, and an illuminating one." Solowey let the moment dazzle, his eyes twinkling enjoyment over the suspense he was creating. "From what has been discovered so far, Buloff has more sides to his personality than a chameleon. He's used the following aliases." He referred to a palm-sized notebook. "Werner Bacher, Matthieu Kober, and Erik Jagendorf. Before his present impersonation of salvationist and missionary, he was, successively, a director of a nudist colony in Ulster County, a chiropractor with a mail-order diploma in medicine obtained from a college which the federal authorities have since closed down and prosecuted, and a detective."

"A detective!"

"An insurance-company detective. The Centralia Underwriters, a Delaware corporation." Solowey looked slyly at Devereaux. "My operative was alive to the possibilities of his research. He at once plunged into a spot check of that Ulster County colony."

"No good." Devereaux's hand gestured impatiently. "It's a waste of time and money. Have him spot-check Buloff's tie-up with that insurance company instead. That's obviously the best bet."

"I did." Solowey broke into a wide smile. "I sent him to the Centralia Underwriters and spoiled his fun." The portly detective chuckled. "I promised he could resume with Ulster County if the insurance phase of Buloff's past proved a disappointment."

"I want a complete story," Devereaux said seriously, disdaining the comedy. "A detailed record of every operation Buloff, or Jagendorf, was involved in for the company. I want the history of every case, naming names, places, et cetera. I want it in chronological order, covering the whole term of Buloff's employment."

Solowey looked into Devereaux's face earnestly. "Building hopes?"

"Building to a letdown, maybe." Devereaux grimaced. "How'd your operative dredge up all that Buloff memoranda?"

"From a fortuitous beer with a city editor. Coulter, our operative, was in MacManus's Bowery Tavern, undoubtedly intending to drown his failures vis-à-vis Buloff. The tavern is a block or two from the Old New York Mission. Coulter joined the city editor in a beer, asked a question about Buloff idly, expecting nothing, and obtained a windfall. The newspaperman remembered an incident long in the past involving Buloff—alias Dr. Matthieu Kober, Chiropractor, with a mail-order diploma from a purported McKinley-Polk College of Evansville, Indiana." Solowey stopped, chuckling.

"What was the incident?"

"A criminal complaint lodged against Buloff in New York County in 1936 by an Eva Wolfast. Eva Wolfast charged that Buloff, as Kober, representing himself as a doctor, had performed a chiropractic abortion on her in Dayton, Ohio, in 1931; that in tampering with her spine, he had left her with a partial disability of one of her limbs."

"How did Eva Wolfast catch up with Buloff five years later, and in another state?"

"An unexpected encounter. Buloff was coming along a street, and they came face to face. Eva Wolfast recognized him."

"What happened to her complaint?"

"First Buloff denied everything, then fought extradition, and finally posted a bond with the Ohio court. The case was postponed four times, and then dismissed for lack of corroborating evidence. Our man, Coulter, acting on the tip obtained over MacManus's bar, did his research on Buloff by telephone, from the Ohio court files. They had done an investigation of Buloff, preliminary to indicting him."

"What was the sequence of aliases? With which activity did each go?"

"Werner Bacher, nudist colony. Matthieu Kober, Doctor of Chiropractics. Erik Jagendorf, detective."

"Erik Jagendorf, then, came *after* the other two."

"Yes."

"How did his stint as Erik Jagendorf become a matter of record in the Buloff-Kober versus Eva Wolfast complaint?"

"Buloff let Erik Jagendorf become part of the record by choice. In arguing against the move to indict him, he used his one valid reference, his term as Erik Jagendorf, insurance detective. He even filed character and achievement affidavits attested to by a Centralia vice-president."

Devereaux nodded thoughtfully. "It was all there, buried in Ohio Court records, almost beyond resurrection."

"Just the accident of a beer in the right place, at the right time, with the *one* man," Solowey said thankfully, "or Buloff would be a man of mystery, like the others."

"An accident, sure," Devereaux observed. "But a good piece of successful sleuthing is *the* lucky accident. Ask a detective."

Solowey smiled. "I'll tell myself. I once caught a bigamist by taking the wrong train."

"Let's not overcapitalize Buloff's case history, yet. The lucky accident might very well turn out to have no informational bearing on Buloff as he relates to our case.

"Funny thing," Devereaux mused aloud a moment later. "Buloff, with his aliases and shady background, getting by the parole board as custodian of Longo's freedom!"

"A blunder, Devereaux. And an honest one, probably. Buloff's biography wasn't available to the board. They just saw him as the head of the Old New York Mission."

"Funny evolution for Buloff—playing salvationist."

"It isn't so funny, Devereaux. In fact, I can make a convincing psychiatric argument for Buloff living exactly the role we find him in."

"Don't bother making it." Devereaux grinned good-naturedly. "Anything more on Phillips?"

"Just what I read in the papers. Nothing more." Solowey picked a newspaper off his desk and chuckled. "Our esteemed critic has become even more acid in the last days. Listen." The portly detective inclined toward a marked out paragraph on the theater page. " 'The most engaging acts in last night's *Second Breakfast* were the intermissions. In Mary Lou Foster, ingénue, medical science has found a quite revolutionary substitute for anesthesia.' "

Devereaux went to the door. "How long until a report on that spot check of Buloff's work with the insurance company?"

"An hour, if the operative is diligent. It is merely a matter of getting a transcript."

"If it's an hour, get it to me at the Attic Circus. Otherwise, I'll keep phoning you."

Solowey nodded and gestured toward the window. "What are your plans for Buloff meanwhile?"

Devereaux hesitated. "I'm not sure any more. I'd like him tailed to wherever he hides out, but who'll do it? You've got nobody here, and I want you right at that phone."

"Why not arrest Buloff?"

"On what charge?"

"Material witness to the murder of Longo. Falsification of affidavits representing himself to the parole board as a citizen of unimpeachable standing."

"It's an idea," Devereaux said unenthusiastically.

"It is safety against a repetition of some attempt on you."

Devereaux smiled gratefully. "Thanks for the concern. But just between us, I don't think it's my destiny to be snuffed out by Buloff. I knew that when my good angel had that right front wheel fall off first last night."

"Not your destiny." Solowey picked at Devereaux's observation scoffingly. "I promise you precisely such an ironic engraving on your tombstone. Heroics aside, I strongly urge that you arrest Buloff."

Devereaux grinned and opened the door. "I might. I'll think it over on the way down."

Downstairs, a jam of traffic formed a wall hiding the south side of Forty-second Street. The lights changed, the vehicles began to crawl, and Devereaux stared intensely through the free spaces between the moving vehicles. He crisscrossed the street in the erratic style of jaywalking, and reached the safety of the opposite curb one movement faster than a racing crosstown bus.

The blue sedan that had been parked parallel with the White Rose Bar was gone.

CHAPTER TWELVE

1.

The taut lines in his face dissolved, as if warmed by his thinking, and a light smile hovered around his mouth. Cute kid, he whispered admiringly, and conjured up Jennifer in his mind's eye. She was riding the curve of the moon clad in a dancer's leotard. Damned cute kid, he repeated possessively, out loud, like a man challenging the opinion of another and the blue-nosed world around. He caught himself wanting to shout a defiant "Maybe I'll marry her." But his lips were a suddenly sealed frontier, and the thought flew back into his head, to buzz there like a bumblebee trapped in a windowless and doorless room.

He was alone in the Buick, moving at a snail's pace, en route to the Attic Circus.

A tower clock somewhere boomed twelve. He had an impulse to hum, and he frowned, sacking his memory files for a suitable number. Music had been a neglected medium with him, all his years long. Finally, his improvised da-de-da-da-da became something identifiable, and Devereaux's expression grew a shade crestfallen. I ought to be woo-hooing at Clara Bow, he told himself ruefully. He had been humming a bar from *Avalon*, a song popular circa 1925.

He pulled to the curb on the avenue just around the corner from the Attic Circus, window-shopped, then let an impulse whip him into a haberdashery shop.

From a display rack he selected a multi-toned silk cravat, with yellow predominating as a color motif, like a monk suddenly daring the colors of the world. He unknotted his drab blue tie, dropped it into a wastebasket, donned the new purchase, then started for the Attic Circus on foot.

Sadye's pouting mouth on the sidewalk poster was missing. Devereaux tried the door of the Attic Circus mechanically, then rattled the doorknob as he reread the lettered sign set on the inside of the glass door as if rejecting its message. The sign read: *Closed Tuesdays*.

He had turned away, wondering where a pugilist turned restaurateur might be found on his free day, when the familiar blue sedan suddenly loomed in his vision. Buloff's car stood across the street. It was parked and unoccupied, but it clamored at Devereaux like a live thing. He had missed spotting it in his approach.

The detective walked a few paces below the restaurant door, worked the slide handle of an iron Florentine gate that led into an alleyway, then moved quietly into the depths of the alley. He turned into an el, and his mind constructed a blueprint of the club interior while he matched each ground-floor window he passed with its location on his blueprint.

He found the windows of Lippy's rear office-studio, stopped, then went back over his visualized blueprint to check the accuracy of his decision. The leaded glass windows before him were Lippy's private club quarters. He was certain of it.

Devereaux flattened against the brick building wall, edged noiselessly toward a window with his head on an elevation just inches above the sill, and listened intensely. Moments passed, and his senses were martialed into one sensitized receiving set, but there was no pickup. The room behind the window was a blank, dead area. He put hands to the unlocked window, paused, looked around him with involuntary guilt, then began to raise it slowly. When the window was raised about a foot, he stopped, listened, then peered in.

The interior was gloom-shadowed. The outside daylight still in his eyes like the glare of a flash bulb made the inside gloom heavier and the shadows deeper. There were no sounds, no reaction in the room, and Devereaux decided it was untenanted. If Latimer or Buloff, or both, were in the club, compatibly or in opposition, they were elsewhere than in Lippy's private quarters. He raised the window higher, this time more boldly, and climbed into the room.

He was stock-still, just inside the room, adjusting his sight, when there was a sudden, close, deafening sound, like a rush of water against his eardrums. The blow toppled him over. He sat on the floor askew, in a momentary paralysis but conscious, and felt rather than saw a vaulting silhouette vanish through the open window. Soon he was back on his feet in a rising wave, then out in the alley with his gun drawn and pointing.

The alleyway was empty. There were no sounds of retreating feet. A medley of street noises pulsed through the alley. There was a throbbing hum of machinery from a power plant somewhere. A dog barked once in an adjoining yard.

Beyond the iron Florentine gate, a flow of pedestrians moved against each other. Across the street, an R. H. Macy electric delivery wagon filled the place quitted by Buloff's blue sedan. Devereaux looked up the street vainly. The blue sedan had pulled away and vanished. The blow in Lippy's private quarters had immobilized him just long enough.

Devereaux climbed back through the window. He was dry right to the base of his throat and a sense of portent was a boulder in his stomach.

In the far corner of the room, deep in the shadows, he found Lippy on the floor propped against a wall. His knees were higher than his head, as if a barrier against a sudden assault. The head was tipped forward slightly, and the mouth was agape, as if Lippy were choked up with a mouthful of unspoken words.

Devereaux looked at the figure moodily for a long time, then removed his hat in a slow, mechanical reaction to the sublimity of death.

2.

An hour later, Devereaux pushed through the street door of the Attic Circus; he was flanked by Captain Anders and Solowey. Anders was saying, "I want the whole story, Johnny, every word of it, in triplicate, and all of it over your signature." His fingers pressed into Devereaux's arm. "You'll also have to put your reinstatement papers into the works right away, so that you can copper with more warrant than the Department's sentimental feeling about you."

Anders' voice jumped a notch. "Three stiffs, Johnny. I ask you! You can't play solitaire behind Solowey's license with the Department watching from the sidelines. Dammit, blind faith goes just so far. There'll be one helluva hue and cry about Latimer. I can't just say an ex-champ has been killed mysteriously and then go about other business. A million people who saw him fight will be screaming for revenge."

Anders dabbed a handkerchief along his brow, cheeks, and neck. "And the Summit police have been driving me crazy with telephone calls. The newspapers have been riding the hell out of them over Castle." They stood massed on the sidewalk. "Johnny, get my point?"

Devereaux sighed heavily and nodded agreement. Anders read his face suspiciously, satisfying himself, then went back into the club.

The street was a forest of police cars cutting into the curb at odd angles. An improvised police line manned a precarious free space just outside the Attic Circus door. Crowds pushed forward in little experimental feelers of strength, and then ebbed away. Reporters with press cards in their hatbands, officials, and some men lugging camera equipment fought through into the free space and then disappeared into the depths of the club.

Across the street, on a window-sized score sheet that provided an inning-by-inning account of the baseball contest between the New York Giants and the Philadelphia Athletics as a public service donored by Joe's Delicatessen, an aproned waiter was writing in bold capitals, LIPPY LATIMER DEAD. The grapevine had eclipsed the newspaper and radio in spot news coverage.

Devereaux linked arms with Solowey. "My car's around the corner."

Solowey panted with Devereaux's racing stride. "Sad about Latimer," he puffed. "Of sports I know nothing, yet even to me he was a legendary figure."

"Uh-huh," Devereaux agreed huskily. "It was the end of an era when that bullet dropped him. They'll be hanging crepe on Broadway."

"Buloff shot him?"

Devereaux said nothing, letting a picture construct itself in his mind.

"How long had Latimer been dead?" Solowey asked.

"Thirty or so minutes, at the most, by the time the medical examiner got there. Deduct the twenty minutes it took Doc Willis to get to the club, and Lippy had been shot not more than fifteen minutes before I arrived there."

"The time element fits," Solowey said. "Buloff pulled away from outside the White Rose Bar and went after Latimer. The distance is less than five minutes to the Attic Circus. He had all the time he needed to shoot Latimer, but not enough time to escape before you climbed in that window."

Devereaux nodded guardedly. "Even so, if Buloff did it he didn't try to make a prompt getaway. He had a total time of up to fifteen minutes before I came in the window."

Solowey shrugged. "Maybe he had no feeling of haste. After all, the club was closed to intruders, and he knew you were safely occupied back in my office. Maybe he delayed because he was looking for something."

"*If* it was Buloff," Devereaux said. "I don't mean to quibble, but a fact is a fact, and even the coincidence of time, opportunity, the sneak assault on me, and Buloff's car parked outside, doesn't prove that he was the triggerman. Buloff might have found Latimer dead, just as I did."

Devereaux unlocked the Buick. They sat wordlessly for a while, then Devereaux said, "Longo, Castle, Latimer, Buloff, and Phillips." His voice marveled, "A weird, mismatched quintet. A half-literate ex-boxer, a perfumed critic, a hate publisher, an ex-insurance detective turned salvationist, and a cheap dip. What made an odd assortment like that dance to the same tune?"

Solowey observed dryly, "Your mismatched quintet is a duet now. Phillips and Buloff. And one of them is your killer." He added as an afterthought, "Unless there is a sixth person we have not encountered yet."

Devereaux's eyes kindled, and he turned the idea over in his mind. "A sixth party," he said half-aloud. "Out to kill the other five to shut them up?"

"It's possible." Solowey arched a look at his colleague. "In the tumult of everything, you've forgotten your first interest in the case."

"Funny," Devereaux said, "but Jennifer Phillips seems a curious irrelevance now. No bearing on the case whatsoever, as it shapes up."

Solowey was shaking his head, and Devereaux said hurriedly, "Get what I mean, Solowey. For us, Jennifer Phillips poses one question: Is or is not Martin Phillips her father? Period. Our negative findings there so far, the lack of any concrete data that prove their relationship, and the peculiar character of the girl's story about him, plus Phillips' peculiarity generally more than hint that he isn't. So much for that."

Devereaux paused and a frown cut across his brow. "From

the moment I went into Cora Jennings' room, with each development as the circle grew wider and wider, the sheer problem of Jennifer Phillips became more incidental, something far less than the complex of conspiracy and murder we found ourselves submerged in."

"I don't quite follow," Solowey said. "Are you actually detaching Jennifer Phillips and the question of her parentage from the case as a whole?"

"Not exactly." Devereaux sounded uncertain. "I just mean that I can't imagine a real connection between the girl and the rest of it. Suppose we say arbitrarily that Martin Phillips is not her father. So much for that, and solved, and period. But we still have five principals in a murder story—three dead and two alive. We still have a puzzle, and we're still pig blind about what it all means."

Solowey was shaking his head doubtfully, and Devereaux's tone quickened. "You're about to remind me that the girl's story was the touchstone for everything that happened subsequently. That my visit to Cora Jennings' room and the violence from then on became part of my experience because the girl approached me with a story one night."

Solowey nodded, and Devereaux continued, "Okay, granted. But even if the girl had never come to me that first night, Longo would have been there, in the Hotel Orleans, rifling a dead woman's effects the next day. And whatever existed between Phillips, Castle, Latimer, and Buloff would ferment and ferment and sooner or later explode into murder. Suppose even that Phillips *is* the girl's father. What would be different? What could—"

Devereaux stopped, suddenly at a loss. A neglected fact had suddenly flashed through his head. Longo had been rifling Cora Jennings' effects. And Cora Jennings had been the remembered housemother of a home for waifs in Jennifer's story.

Devereaux's lips pursed. He'd been setting up his own blindspot. The case, in its every ramification, ran together.

He couldn't detach the girl from the welter. He couldn't set her problem aside, or her, as an isolated thing, something without roots in the holocaust of murder.

He sighed gigantically. "Okay. Hasty conclusions aren't conclusions, and we've got a whole continent of hills to climb. Got that schedule on Buloff as Jagendorf the insurance detective with you?"

Solowey nodded, fussed in an inside coat pocket, then handed Devereaux a sheaf of folded pages.

Devereaux opened the pages, scanned them once, then over again. "A lot of stuff, for two short years of activity." He ran a finger up and down the pages, computing rapidly. "The man was a beaver. Thirty-one cases, about, covering the whole range of insurance frauds, and involving individuals and companies." He shook his head and groaned. "No good to us. We'd need six months to check into all of them."

"Not all of them," Solowey corrected. "Just the big ones. Just where the stakes were big."

"Still a colossal project. More than a dozen on this list qualify." Devereaux shook his head. "This is one time I'm giving thoroughness the go-by. Too arduous, and besides, I can't afford to subsidize all that research."

"And nothing might come of it, anyhow. Buloff's past as an insurance detective might have no significance at all." Solowey smiled. "Perhaps it is better that you think economically."

Devereaux folded the pages carefully and put them in his pocket. "Hope my idea of thrift isn't a costly mistake," he said anxiously. "There might be a clue somewhere in those cases cheap at any price." He fidgeted moodily for a moment, then shrugged anxiety away and turned the ignition key.

"You have a destination?" Solowey asked.

"I have." Devereaux worked the wheel, and honked his horn in warning. "Criminal Court. We're checking back into their files. There's a case I want to find out about and forget." He smiled. "For the sake of thoroughness, and especially since the investment there requires only your time and mine."

Entering the downtown district, Solowey inquired, "What case are we checking into?"

"The People of the State of New York versus Frankie Hughes. An armed robbery and second-degree murder conviction that got Hughes sentenced to sixty years."

Devereaux eased the Buick into the curb. "Frankie Hughes was the only casualty in the Big House during Longo's stay there. Hughes suffered a dizzy spell while under a hot shower. He was scalded to death."

Solowey looked puzzled. "That means something?"

"Probably not. The Warden and all his little men wrote it off as an accidental combination of a man subject to fainting spells, and faulty prison plumbing. I'm just proceeding on the general premise that Longo had some purpose in getting arrested that day outside the Paddock Café. Some reason for wanting to be sent up."

Devereaux looked into Solowey's frowning countenance. "You don't see it at all, huh?"

"I see it as just monotonous and unrewarding hours with records," Solowey said reproachfully. "And such an anemic little lead!" He wagged a rebuking finger. "Thoroughness, bah. You are letting your passion for the smallest details lead you around by the nose."

CHAPTER THIRTEEN

1.

The record room was airless and had the heavy, tomblike quiet common to libraries. Bars of sunlight hung stiffly in the air, like drab dusty-gray streamers.

An elderly clerk with exaggerated sideburns came up to Devereaux's table. "The People of the State of New York versus Frankie Hughes," he announced, and set the dossier at the detective's elbow.

Devereaux arranged his chair to exploit the bare light and plunged into reading, oblivious to his companion.

Solowey's cough beside him was an unmistakably eloquent rebuke. "I am as superfluous here as a third arm, my friend." The portly detective grunted to his feet. "If it were merely a nervous need for companionship with you—"

Devereaux poked the rolling stomach placatingly, and tendered to Solowey the topmost pages he had already completed. "Read with me. The wrong track for us, probably, but the stuff's absorbing. The individual versus society, and with more of a bang than you ever find in fiction. Frankie Hughes was just a twenty-year-old kid when he pulled the payroll job."

Solowey looked disposed to bicker, but sat down like a man compromising his good common sense. "I should read crime histories just to pass the time," he grumbled.

Devereaux leafed through the file quickly, seeking an outline notion of its scope. The orderly sequences told the short and cheerless story of a youth, born perversely, predoomed, and the crime that brought him to judgment. There was the terse police story of the crime and apprehension, the probation officer's report couched in quasi-sociological phrasing, and the summary story of the trial and the punishment.

Devereaux returned to systematic word reading. He read page 4, then over again slowly. It seemed oddly more telling, of greater significance, than what he had drawn from it. He scanned the page again, dimly conscious of something standing just outside his recognition. The page blurred and his eyes began to burn. He closed his eyes for a few seconds, then opened them and repeated the page once more, now certain that something overlooked or shunted was clamoring at the door of his consciousness.

He narrowed the area by reading details, estimating them, then dismissing them. Soon he read and reread a single sentence with growing vexation, while the suspicion formed and grew in his mind that his imagination was playing tricks.

The puzzling sentence was bald, factual, without subtlety or hinted meanings, easily understood. He read it again, with his lips, half to himself. "The messenger left the Bank of Manhattan with the weekly payroll of the Hubbell Electrical Appliance Company and proceeded on foot one block to . . ."

Solowey's eyes were trained on him questioningly. Devereaux stared back for a moment that grew and hung aimlessly in time before meaning burst into his mind.

Devereaux's sudden elation infused Solowey. "You found a link!" the portly detective exclaimed.

"I hit the jackpot!" Devereaux drew a deep, thankful breath, like a man miraculously rescued from dark waters. He reached into his pocket and brought out the folded onionskin sheath.

"Read this first," Devereaux ordered, drawing a nail line

under the sentence that had obdurately haunted his thinking.

Solowey complied, and Devereaux unfolded the onionskins and searched out an entry.

"Now," Devereaux crowed, "for the stitch that proves coming here was an example of thrift right out of *Poor Richard's Almanac*." He drew a nail line under an entry on the onionskin, and waited triumphantly for Solowey's reaction.

"The Hubbell Electrical Appliance Company." There was a comical note of awe in Solowey.

"Check. Frankie Hughes stole their payroll and shot their messenger. Buloff, as Jagendorf, was the insurance-company detective assigned to the case." Devereaux looked solemnly at Solowey. "Know what I'm thinking?"

Solowey nodded. "That Buloff double-crossed his own company, that he went after the spoils himself. That Longo was his agent."

"And that Longo got into Sing Sing to kill Frankie Hughes. That explains a habitual pickpocket suddenly in the toils for gun toting."

"The deduction has substance enough," Solowey observed cautiously. "But the elapsed twenty years. What could be the explanation for that?"

Devereaux shook his head slowly. "And there are other questions, too. When did Buloff cut himself in, or gobble it all? Was he in on the original conspiracy to stick up that payroll messenger? Did he inspire it by fingering the job? Did he come in *after* the robbery, when he tumbled to the facts while investigating it? Or did he tumble twenty years later and go after Frankie Hughes on the theory that Frankie had the money cached somewhere? Remember, the money was never recovered, as far as I've read."

Solowey said thoughtfully, "You're suggesting that Longo's assignment as Buloff's plant was to pump Hughes, discover the whereabouts of the hidden money, and then kill Hughes."

"It's an idea," Devereaux said, "and I've turned it over in my mind before. But let's finish the case file, huh? Maybe we can trim the guesswork down even more." He returned to page 5, passing each page to Solowey as he completed reading it.

The dusty-gray streamers were gone and amber ceiling lights flooded the room when Devereaux was finally disposed to renewed conversation.

"We're a lot smarter for having wandered in here, Solowey," Devereaux observed soberly. He beamed fondly at his portly colleague. "This one paid off, but remind me to bore you sometime with an account of the thousands of man-hours I've wasted running fragments of leads into a big, inky void."

Solowey smiled sheepishly. "I suppose I should eat crow for the disparagement I heaped upon you for coming here."

Devereaux grinned broadly. "I'll not insult you with a fake show of modesty." He pushed the file away, signaling to the elderly clerk with exaggerated sideburns.

"Come on." Devereaux rose to his feet. "I've got a hollow in my stomach that needs filling. We'll grab a bite somewhere, and go over what we've learned."

2.

The workingmen massed around the bar at Reardon's Bar and Grill had the oddly bewitched look of men star-gazing in the deep night. They were looking raptly at an eight-foot television screen tooled into a shelf high above eye level. A wrestling match was being televised.

Off in a booth, Devereaux and Solowey were intimately hunched in conversation, dead to their surroundings.

A girl with a saucily painted mouth set twin plates down on their table with a clatter.

"Franks and beans," she announced superfluously. She caught Devereaux's eye coquettishly, then, finding no answer, minced away.

The pair fell to emptying their plates swiftly and silently in an undeclared but tacit moratorium on talk.

"The hundred-thousand-dollar loot was never recovered," Devereaux began in a gulping delivery. He raised his glass of water and took a long, relieving swallow. "And Hughes' confederates on the job were never identified and brought to book. Hughes didn't inform on them, and the police accomplished nothing except sending Hughes up the river."

"A remarkable display of loyalty, Hughes', particularly in view of the judge's remarks and the conditions to the sentence he imposed."

Devereaux nodded. "More than loyalty or the aping of the so-called gangland code of silence; it was the stuff of martyrdom. The sentence was shrewdly designed to break Hughes' morale, sooner or later, and get him to sing out." He thought about it. A total of sixty years, on three separate counts. Three separate twenty-year sentences, running consecutively, with the stipulation that Hughes be brought back before the court after each sentence, after each twenty years, and be given the opportunity of mitigating his punishment by confessing the whole truth.

Devereaux's face drew solemnly. "Hughes would have to be crazy to keep playing patsy for the rest of his life, just to keep faith with his pals outside."

"Crazy or the pathological martyr type, as you implied previously," Solowey said.

Devereaux calculated swiftly. "The first twenty-year sentence was about over. The pressure on Hughes to sing must have been terrific."

"The pressure on his compatriots outside to prevent Hughes' singing undoubtedly was even more terrific." Solowey looked at Devereaux keenly. "The accidental death by scalding was a– ah– providential development."

"Or the successful outcome of some pretty desperate plotting."

"Longo," Solowey said.

Devereaux nodded. "Longo, pretty clearly now. He bided his time in Sing Sing and disposed of Frankie Hughes in what looked for all the world like the perfect crime."

"Longo as agent for Buloff and others." Solowey looked across at Devereaux. "Who are the others and how many others?"

Devereaux was lost in his thinking. The reply that had leaped to his lips was a stunning simplification.

"The others could be our whole cast of principals, those dead and those alive," Devereaux said slowly, as if deliberateness acquitted him of arbitrariness. "And the most reasonable assumption about Buloff now is that he somehow came into the deal sometime *after* the payroll robbery and shooting. As a blackmailer, or self-declared partner, after having scouted the case and solved it as an insurance-company operative."

Solowey nodded in tentative agreement. "It makes a plausible picture." His eyes wandered away to the television screen. The wrestling match was over, and an indistinct comedy short resurrected from movie archives had replaced it. Mustachioed Keystone cops were falling all over the landscape.

Solowey chuckled appreciatively and nudged his colleague. Devereaux stared blankly at the screen without moving a facial muscle. "Wrong time for laughter," he said, pulling Solowey back to the tête-à-tête.

"You should learn to mix grimness with equal parts of humor," Solowey smiled, clucking his tongue. "The mind needs it, like the body needs a balanced diet."

"Back to cases, huh?" Devereaux insisted unyieldingly.

"Cases, then," Solowey sighed. "We have achieved a skeleton outline into which you have fitted an imposing cast of characters, my good Devereaux. Now it remains to document your story, before you can reasonably expect to sell it. How do you propose to go about documenting the story?"

Devereaux hesitated and Solowey suggested, "You could

arrest Phillips and examine him. And Buloff, too. Confronted with what you already know, one or the other must give in."

Solowey added, "As a ruse, you could perhaps play one against the other. The psychological possibilities are immense, especially since one of them is doubtlessly the murderer."

"The suggestion's okay," Devereaux said. "Third degree and psychological skulduggery may be the inevitable end tactic. But first I'll continue along methodical lines and see what new padding I can find for that skeletonized outline." His tone became matter of fact. "You get down to Captain Anders' office, borrow his stenographer, and get off a detailed résumé of what we've been up to and what we've discovered, from scratch up to the present." Devereaux smiled faintly, "Do that before Anders drops a kidney. Also, get Anders to flash an arrest-on-sight order for Buloff."

"And Phillips," Solowey supplemented.

Devereaux shook his head. "Leave Phillips to me. For a while, anyhow." A curiously uncertain note crept into his voice. "I imagine Phillips needs handling."

"Surgery is a better word," Solowey said wisely. "And you will need to be infinitely adept with scalpel to cut Phillips from the girl without cutting the girl just a little."

"If there was some damned way," Devereaux said restlessly. "I hate to see the notoriety touch her, shake her up."

Solowey regarded his colleague with warm eyes. "This tender concern for the girl, Devereaux," he said approvingly. "I like it. I like very much the Devereaux who is more than just a policeman." A smile filled the moon face. "Love liberates the half of you that you keep under stern lock and key, my friend."

"Go to hell, you goddam overstuffed Cupid," Devereaux said.

"You are new to sentiment," Solowey said serenely. "And understandably awkward in it. But it suits you, Devereaux.

128

It suits you better than you know." He nodded his head. "Phillips will be left to you. And the Lord grant you have the ability to detach the girl from the notoriety, even if you have to compromise your police oath just a little."

A frown darkened Devereaux's face. Solowey got to his feet. "Where is the invincible Devereaux method taking you from here?" he inquired in a patently forced effort at humor.

Devereaux replied eagerly, as if glad for a reprieve from the mood of his thinking, "To the Rogue's Gallery for a print of Frankie Hughes' face. Then home for that night-club photograph of Castle and Phillips. Then somewhere for a still of Lippy Latimer. With all that, I'm off to the neighborhood listed as Frankie Hughes' last address in the court file. I'll reconnoiter, inquire around, and see if I can make a pretty sound but still somewhat hypothetical story do a convincing imitation of life."

Solowey bowed in a clownish effect of idol worship.

3.

Click, click. The high heels were harsh on the sidewalk. He sensed it to be Jennifer before she overtook him.

"I waited hoping you'd be coming along, Johnny."

"Nice doorstep surprise." He smiled warmly.

"Johnny, I've got to talk to you," she said urgently.

She was wan and solemn to his probing look. Morale, as much as she could have had, was evaporating with the mists in her eyes.

"Inside," he gestured, jingling his key ring.

They climbed the short stoop to the Argyle Studios, Non-Housekeeping Apartments.

"Some coffee while we talk," Devereaux said. "Then I've got to run."

He filled an electric percolator with water drawn from a bathroom tap, then poured raw coffee in over the water by eye measure from a grocery can stored in a bureau drawer.

"My one secret culinary skill." Devereaux smiled. He plugged the percolator into a wall socket. "Funny thing, but what comes out tastes like coffee."

The levity glanced off. She was dead white; very small and lost in the depths of an overstuffed chair.

Her speech stung him suddenly. It came like a blunt-edged missile shot from the springs of the chair.

"Johnny, give it up!"

"Give it up!" Devereaux repeated blankly, as if the sense of her outcry eluded him. He watched her come to his side.

"Yes, Johnny. Give it up."

Her fingers were through his sleeve, hot on his flesh.

"It's no good, Johnny, no good," she was babbling. "I saw the new headline today. Latimer. Dead, murdered. So many murders. I'll read about you, too. Murdered." The mists ran into splotches on her cheeks. "Murdered, Johnny! I couldn't stand that. I'd die, too."

For me, Devereaux thought. The scene is for me, he marveled with a choking gladness. It's the scene women make over men, over *the* man.

He cupped her chin in his hands. "Your worry over me is the biggest news in my life so far. And thanks awfully. But I take a lot of killing. A hell of a lot of killing."

"Johnny, you must give it up," she said unconsolably.

He shook his head slowly.

"Yes," she insisted. "You must!" Her fingers were back, hard. "I asked you in, Johnny. Now I'm begging you to get out."

"It's gone way past your invitation or you, kid. I told you it had the other night." His tone hardened. "I've never dropped a case." He held her at arm's length, and then added, "I can't. My whole life's against it."

There was a sudden wall between them, and she saw it. "If they kill you, Johnny," she said desperately.

"I'll lose no more than I'd lose if I dropped the case now."

"But you're not a policeman any more. Not really!"

Devereaux said nothing. She looked at him for a while, with her eyes searching every detail of his expression. Soon she understood it. "You are a policeman. All through you, you're a policeman," she said beatenly.

"I'm a bad cook." Devereaux sniffed. There was a smell of burned coffee in the room. He crossed the room and pulled the electric cord from the wall socket.

He watched her take the percolator from him, cleanse it under the bathroom tap, then refill it, as if intent on the sheer mechanical task.

CHAPTER FOURTEEN

1.

The station signs on the Broadway-Brooklyn "L" read: *LORIMER STREET*. The train huffed to a rolling stop. eaux alighted, then began the long descent to the street below.

This branch of the Williamsburg area had the derelict look of an American desert town. The walks were rutted; there were deep pits like the scars of gigantic bombs in countless building lots. The tenanted buildings were old-law, ramshackle, and unsafe. The noise of a dog in some backyard gave a visitor the fleeting impression of the howl of a prairie wolf.

The air felt curiously like the breath of the sick buildings around, the slow-moving elders, the listless young, and the general squalor. It was thin and parched, and it stuck at the base of the throat like a cottony gag.

Devereaux looked about him as if into depths just beyond reach of the eye. The scene was his long-ago boyhood. This slum, exactly and no less, on Chicago's North Side, had saddened and gladdened him, hurt and rallied him, weaned him, branded him, then left him to face the perplexities of manhood and all the years after. Dared him to face them. . . .

He looked around him, bemused. It was the same as the one he had been born to, as all slums were the same. He read

the signs on the store fronts nostalgically, as if greater significance than their mean legend lay in them. ALLIE'S POOL
PARLOR. CHEAP JOE'S, CANDY AND STATION-
ERY. BONURA'S, FRESH FISH. EMPIRE, WINDOW
SHADES AND AWNINGS. THE NEMO, a theater
showing a cowboy Western and the sixth episode of *Death
in Diamonds.*

Right out of my memory book and brought to life, Devereaux thought to himself. And unchanged, as if a quarter
century were a moment. Would Frankie Hughes, too, find
it unchanged if he could re-enter life and walk these streets,
Devereaux wondered.

An aging cop whose head and body made an L and
whose pants bagged at the knees came toward Devereaux.
The detective eyed him appraisingly. An oldster, pastured
in a ghost town, counting off the minutes until his pen-
sioned retirement.

Devereaux signaled the patrolman and then introduced
himself.

"Maybe you can help me," the detective said dubiously.

The old man backed against the remnant of a fence and
slouched down on his spine with his hands down to his
knees, as if preparing against the drive of a younger man.

"What are you after?" he asked wearily.

"Information about someone who grew up hereabouts
twenty or so years ago."

"Long time ago, twenty years," the patrolman said chid-
ingly.

"Sure, I know." Devereaux smiled. "This your precinct as
far back as that?"

"As far back as ten. Before that I worked out of this precinct some years, and up in Greenpoint other times." The
patrolman shifted his weight. "I came on the force in 1919,
right out of the war," he added complainingly.

"Regret it?" Devereaux inquired.

"I do," the patrolman said, fuming to get it off his chest.

"When an old man like me, only three months away from his pension, is kept on active duty while young squirts sit behind a desk—" He left the sentence unfinished, and the grievance flamed in his chinless face.

"Find this area much different today? Against twenty years ago, I mean," the detective asked.

The patrolman's look slighted Devereaux and the detective said smilingly, "Kids have come of age and stuff like that, I know. What I mean is, what do you find pretty much the same, only older?" He gestured toward CHEAP JOE'S, CANDY AND STATIONERY. "Like that candy store. Does Cheap Joe date back twenty years? And other establishments and neighborhood people. How many of them are still at the same old stand?"

The patrolman rubbed his chin thoughtfully, then squinted questioningly at Devereaux. "Who is this someone you're looking to find out something about?"

"Frankie Hughes," Devereaux replied. "He grew up around here. His last address was 26½ Johnson Avenue. That was in 1928."

A hand flapped loosely, pointing a direction. "26½ Johnson Avenue's three blocks west." The eyes looked mildly curious. "What about Frankie Hughes?"

"He was caught in a payroll holdup that resulted in the death of a messenger. The Hubbell Electrical Appliance Company. Frankie Hughes was convicted and sent to Sing Sing. Remember the case?"

The patrolman shook his head. "They grew more little gangsters around here twenty years ago than you could shake a billy at," he said sourly. "H'isters, rape artists, cop haters. Snotnosed kids carried guns, and every Saturday night was Mardi Gras for the shooting that went on. We used to patrol in teams." A hand flapped loosely. "Allie's Pool Hall there was a big hangout for the little bastards."

Devereaux regarded the patrolman. The old man couldn't

possibly cope with a sudden incident of the streets. "All that's gone today, huh?" he said.

"The neighborhood's tame because it's dead," the patrolman said thankfully. "The big families have broken up, and eighty per cent of the people have moved away." His mouth crooked rakishly. "And sixty per cent of them are no doubt dead and buried by now."

Devereaux nodded distractedly. "Does Allie's Pool Hall have the same ownership today?"

The patrolman's head went up and down affirmatively. "Only Allie's not the same man today he was twenty years ago. Used to be a king lording it over the young snotnoses who dropped in to play pool and talk over jobs they were going to pull off. What the kids didn't know yet, Allie taught them." The mouth crooked. "Jewish kids called the joint *Cheder* and the Gentile kids called it 'Church.'"

Devereaux grinned. On Chicago's North Side, they had called the pool hall "College."

"Any other oldsters around, like Allie? Someone who would have a close knowledge of kids and their families?"

The patrolman's face emptied and his expression grew momentarily vacant. "There's old Grandma McBride," he said after a while. "Her son ran the funeral parlor at 41½ Johnson Avenue until he passed away with pneumonia five years ago. Grandma keeps the place spic and span, ready for business, just as if Bill was still alive." The patrolman tapped his forehead. "She's dippy. Keeps insisting Bill's sure to come back and be wanting to get right back into action. But if anybody can tell you anything, it's Grandma. She's close on to eighty, about the oldest citizen around."

"Where does she live?"

"In the rear room, back of the funeral parlor." The mouth crooked again. "You can't miss finding the place. There's a casket with silver handles plunked right in the window that Grandma's reserving specially for herself."

"Will she talk to strangers?" Devereaux asked anxiously.

"At the drop of a hat. And quicker than that if you bring her a box of peppermints." A hand motioned cautioningly. "But don't let on you're a cop. Cops, landlords, and anybody from the gas company can't get the time of day around here. Everybody figures we only mean trouble. Everybody from babies sucking at their mother's tit to eighty-year-old Grandma McBride."

Devereaux nodded understandingly. Squalor bred its own curious morality and superstition. "Anybody else you can suggest as a lead?"

"There's the barber on the Meserole Street corner. But Vincente's hearing is gone. You'd go nuts carrying on a conversation with him." The patrolman paused reflectively. "You could hop over to the station house. Keeley there used to be sergeant of the precinct."

Devereaux shook his head. "The police got nowhere twenty years ago. The record shows that pretty clearly. Frankie Hughes had pals, and the case against him was open and shut, yet the police never came up with another arrest after nabbing Hughes." The detective smiled faintly. "Like you said, nobody around here ever gave the police the time of day."

"Cop haters, from the cradle to the grave," the patrolman said resentfully. "Chase a squalling snotnose into a tenement in the old days, and it was like you were in an armed camp. Thirty-six families were ganged up against the law in a minute. Buckets of slop caught you flush coming up the stairs, and bottles beaned you going down. And when the kid grew up, he began to tote a gun, with your name scratched on the first bullet." The patrolman groaned to an erect position. "Good thing the neighborhood's dead as it is these days. I couldn't stand up against it the way it used to be for a minute."

Devereaux smiled sympathetically, then extracted an envelope from an inside pocket. He held a photograph out to the patrolman. "This was the last picture taken of Frankie Hughes. It was taken in Sing Sing. Know him?"

The patrolman regarded it blankly. "No."

Devereaux tendered other photographs to the patrolman. "Do these pictures recall somebody to you?"

The patrolman examined them in turn, then over again.

"Study their expressions, around the forehead and eyes mainly," Devereaux advised. "Try to visualize them as twenty years or so younger."

The patrolman grimaced. "You want me to see men in their forties as youngsters just about ready for their first shave!" He handed the photographs back. "Maybe if you had a magic mirror handy," he added with faint but unmistakable derision.

Devereaux restored the photographs to the envelope and then to his pocket. "An arrow in the air sometimes," he began edgily, than left the justification unfinished. Silly, defending his method to a senile cop whose uniform was just a whimsicality! "Thanks for all the talk," he said finally.

"You're welcome to it."

The detective watched him drag down the street like a sad old mule pulling a load, and a grin began that widened across his face. The command talk had evidently drained the aging patrolman for the day. After a minute, he followed in the patrolman's path, then turned into a side entrance to Allie's Pool Hall.

2.

The pool hall was a square, barnlike store housed in a rotting one-story frame building. The room held two rows of pool tables, six to a side, and all beaten-looking and antique, with the green baize closer to blue and surface tears held in place by strips of Scotch tape in a homemade repair. There was a Coca-Cola box on the side of one wall, and beside it was a slide-window confectionery counter with an old-style cash register on top of it. Framed lithographs scattered along the walls were indiscernible behind dust-caked glass. A calendar advertising a coal company also advertised a gleaming life-sized nude. A sign warned: MINORS UNDER EIGHTEEN KEEP OUT. Another sign admonished: PLEASE REFRAIN FROM USING OBSCENE LANGUAGE. A third sign stipulated rates for several kinds of pool games, and announced in abashed pin-point print: GAMBLING FORBIDDEN.

A man with stringy gray hair that touched the neckband of his grimy, collarless shirt was perched on a high stool near the confectionery counter. His stomach was ballooned out and his hands rested on it in an odd suggestion of piety. He was drowsing.

The pool hall had one other occupant. A boy, barely of age, was practicing improbable shots with ferocious concentration.

Devereaux watched one shot in process. It was a spot shot, with the cueball completing a straight angle and frozen against the far rim of the table. The shot would challenge the wizardry of a champion.

The youth chalked his stick methodically, gave some moments to deliberate, exact measurements of the angle to the pocket, made endless fluid sawing movements with his stick, then thrust forward to make the shot. The stick hit the cueball glancingly, too high, and the ivory ball dribbled forward. A miscue, and a technical scratch—the telltale misplay of an amateur.

A grin flickered across Devereaux's face, and the youth, looking up with a flushing embarrassment, saw it. He glowered, glad to transfer his vexation.

Devereaux crossed the room and nudged the drowsing proprietor. The hands on the ballooned stomach drew apart slowly, and the face came awake.

Blood-speckled eyes brooded at the detective. "Huh?" the man grunted disagreeably.

"Happened to be in the neighborhood, Allie." Devereaux smiled ingratiatingly. "Thought I'd drop in for a chat."

The eyes kindled shrewdly, and Allie took in details of Devereaux's appearance minutely. "Copper," he said accusingly, and turned away.

"Bad guess." Devereaux thought swiftly, then moved to a position facing Allie. "Take a good look," he said, submitting his face.

"I know you?" Allie asked, with his face creased in a straining to remember.

"Mike Devers." Devereaux clapped the pool-hall operator on the shoulder. "It's been a long time, Allie," he said in tones of warm reunion. "More than thirty years since I was a kid on the block." He fixed a palm at an elevation. "I was this high."

Allie shook his head. "Can't place you," he said, extending a limp, moist hand. "So damned many kids. Like a crazy menagerie."

"How's business?" Devereaux said.

"Business!" Allie snorted. "But I don't give a damn. I'm fixed good enough for the few years I'll still be around. What's your racket?"

"Making book," Devereaux said casually.

"Making a buck?" Allie asked, seeking his own independent conclusions with his eyes pricing details of Devereaux's attire.

The detective displayed an expensive ring, quite within Allie's scrutiny. "A dollar here and a dollar there." He smiled modestly.

"Good for you," Allie said with meager approval. "I seen so many of you fart around and never make a connection. Big talk, big schemes, and in the windup"—he spat without saliva—"they don't amount to a spit in the ocean."

"See some of the old gang sometimes?" Devereaux asked idly.

"If they've connected, never. If they're on their asses, they drift around hoping to mooch a couple of bucks." Allie's mouth broke into an ugly grin. "I get postcards all the time from jailbirds asking for smokes and favors for old time's sake."

"I see some of the successful boys around town sometimes," Devereaux said. "Matter of fact, I ran into a couple of them in an uptown night club about a week ago."

"Which of the boys were they?" Allie asked.

"Martie Phillips and Fred Castle." Devereaux's eyes were intent on Allie's expression. "Remember them?"

"Nope. Can't place them," Allie said. He shook his head. "So damned many kids. They used to breed them like flies around here."

"I got a picture of them that night I ran into them." Devereaux fumbled in the envelope without taking it out of his pocket. He fingered the top photograph, remembering its position in the envelope, and drew it out. "A souvenir for my album, for old time's sake," he said, smiling a little foolishly.

Allie stared at the photograph with watering eyes. He opened a cigar box in the candy showcase, found a pair of steel-rimmed eyeglasses, and put them on.

"Nope," he said after a while. "Can't place them at all." A wariness slowly fixed in his face. "So you ran into a couple of the boys. So what?" The early hostility and suspicion were back in his voice. "You just drop around to tell me that?"

"The uptown club was Lippy Latimer's Attic Circus. Classy joint," Devereaux said easily, ignoring the sudden hard vein in Allie. "You remember Lippy, huh? Middleweight champ a while back."

"Latimer was knocked off yesterday," Allie said with his shrewd eyes going over Devereaux anew. "It was in the papers this morning."

"Uh-huh," Devereaux said. "And too bad. **Lippy** was regular. You knew him, huh?"

"I saw him fight in the Garden."

"Sure. But I mean, you saw him around. Before he hit the big time, Lippy was around this neighborhood a lot."

"I wouldn't know," Allie said. "I only saw him fight."

"Lippy used to pal with one of the old gang a lot," Devereaux persisted recklessly. Disarming Allie was obviously impossible, if he wanted to get done what he'd come for. The wily pool-hall operator was a genius at divining motive.

"You don't say!" Allie's brows lifted tauntingly.

"Aren't you curious at all about whom Lippy used to pal around with in the old neighborhood?" Devereaux said.

"No." Allie half-turned away. "Look, Mike Devers, if that's your name, climb back on your bicycle and pedal yourself the hell outa here. You've been piling the shit higher than the ceiling, and it all smells copper just like I figured you when you pushed in here." He picked up a battered magazine and began perusing it.

Devereaux held his ground doggedly, and waited until a hot wave of irritation cooled. "He used to pal around with Frankie Hughes."

Allie's face reacted and his blood-speckled eyes kindled over the magazine.

"Frankie Hughes did a long stretch in Sing Sing, and died there some months ago."

"So?" Allie returned to the tableau unexpectedly.

"Thought you'd quit on me," Devereaux said, puzzled at the sudden evident interest in the pool-hall operator.

"I will quit, and for good, if you don't get to the point."

"What point?" Devereaux said equivocally.

"Your angle," Allie said disgustedly.

"A dollar," Devereaux said. "I've got an idea I'm trying to make good on. If I win, there may be a dollar."

"Thought you said you were a bookmaker."

"I'm still out to make a dollar."

"What are you betting on your chances?" Allie's tongue washed his lower lip and his face stripped the question of its obscurity.

"Fifty," Devereaux said.

Allie became re-absorbed in his magazine reading.

"I'll double it," Devereaux proposed.

Allie looked up disdainfully. "Times five," he said flatly.

"If it's worth it, and if you'll take a check," Devereaux agreed. "I haven't that much in cash."

"That's a cop's trick." Allie made a noise in his throat. "Give me a check and grab me for blackmail."

"Where does blackmail enter it? You've got a right to take money as a fee for co-operating with somebody, anybody." Devereaux found his wallet, and thumbed through the bill compartment. "I've got two hundred and sixty dollars in cash."

"Okay," Allie said. He put his hand out. "I'll co-operate two-sixty's worth." His face broke into an ugly grin. "You can come around for more cash co-operation tomorrow."

Devereaux watched him cram the bills into a pants pocket. "I'm buying a blind package," he said.

"You made your bet," Allie said. He called across the room to the youth busy improving his form and skill. "Hey, Henny."

Henny looked over dutifully.

"Get the hell outa here," Allie said.

The youth lay the cue stick on the table, reached up and shut the light over the table, hoisted his trousers, then strode out.

Allie turned to Devereaux. "I got reason to believe Lippy Latimer was a tough orphan kid who grew up in the Ten Eyck-Bushwick Avenue neighborhood."

"You're sure?"

Allie patted a pants pocket. "I'll bet fifty of the money you gave me I seen Lippy floating around as a kid of maybe fifteen or sixteen. He used to go by the name of Terry—for Terrence. I never knew his other name, but it wasn't Latimer."

"Go on."

"I got reason to believe he put the gloves on for the first time in Marco's Athletic Club, out in East New York. He used the name of Kid Young for a while."

Devereaux nodded to himself. It checked with the lead given Solowey's operative by the San Francisco sportswriter. An involuntary sigh heaved through him. Two principals, Hughes and Latimer, were finally linked to the common background of neighborhood origin.

"What about Frankie Hughes?"

Allie grinned. "I've been asked more questions about Frankie Hughes."

"Who asked you questions about Frankie Hughes?"

"The cops. When Frankie pulled that stickup, there was a regular platoon of cops roaming around the neighborhood asking questions. Just like you're here now asking questions. They closed me down for three months. Even tried to tear up my license to operate." Allie's mouth worked. "On Frankie Hughes your bet doesn't pay off. I can only tell you what I told the cops over and over again twenty years ago. I don't know a damned thing about that Electrical Appliance Company stickup and shooting."

"You could be lying."

Allie shook his head. "If I knew anything, maybe I'd've cashed in on it long ago." His eyes sought Devereaux's shrewdly. "That payroll money never turned up."

"What information have you got about Hughes and Latimer together, teamed up, chumming around maybe?"

"Nothing. Never saw them together. Hughes was just a young punk shooting pool in my place. I never took special notice of him until he made the newspapers."

Devereaux stared at the pool-hall operator. "You could be lying," he said restlessly.

"I'm not. I thought about Latimer and Hughes together long ago. For years I tried to connect them up, but no go." His eyes glinted. "There could have been something in it for me, if I ever did find the connection. Hughes had pals on that job, and the cops turned the neighborhood upside down trying to put a finger on those pals."

"Why were you trying to connect Hughes with Latimer at all? What gave you an idea about Latimer, if you never saw the two together?"

Allie reddened slightly, like a man who'd unguardedly put his foot into it. "I'm talking too much," he said.

"You can't clam up," Devereaux said harshly. "I've got to know."

"I been talking off the top of my head like a young punk!" Allie said disgustedly. "Okay. There was an insurance dick around a few years after Frankie Hughes' trial. He asked me the same questions you're asking. He gave me the idea about Latimer."

"What was the insurance detective's name?" It was a struggle keeping his tone level.

Allie hesitated. "Hagendorf, or some name like it."

Devereaux nodded to himself. Jagendorf-Buloff. Buloff had cut himself a piece of apple pie *after* the original crime. The insurance detective had followed the scent to a black-mail bonanza.

"How much did the insurance detective bet with you?" Devereaux inquired caustically.

Allie kept silent. The answer was as obvious as Allie's petty greeds. Buloff, too, had purchased cash co-operation.

"What about the photograph I showed you—the men I identified as Martin Phillips and Fred Castle?"

"Like I said, I can't place them at all."

"They had other names in their youth," Devereaux suggested.

Allie shook his head. "Can't tell you a thing there. There

were so many damned kids." A pause later he suggested, "Try the schools. There's P. S. 147 over on Siegel and Bushwick. There's a school on Boerum Street, and one on Scholes Street. If they were neighborhood boys, maybe they graduated from somewhere."

Devereaux considered it. "They were all about eighteen or older at the time. Too old for public school."

"There's Eastern District High School over in South Brooklyn. A lot of neighborhood kids travel out to the Hamilton and Erasmus High Schools." Allie laughed shortly. "I'm making like a detective." His eyes glinted. "A detective, like you," he said positively and finally, believing it.

"What about Hughes' people? Where can I find them?"

"Search me. Okay, I've said two-sixty's worth."

Devereaux regarded him quietly. "You said I could come around tomorrow for some more cash co-operation."

"Sure."

"Then you've more to tell."

"Come around and see."

Devereaux balled his hands into fists. Justice, its agent, or somebody owed this bloated conniver a thrashing within an inch of his life. He opened his hands, and the tension left them slowly. The tiny nerves in his hands throbbed and ached for having been denied.

Devereaux went to the front door that opened on Broadway under the "L." He paused outside the plate-glass window momentarily, somehow feeling soiled and defrauded. He arched his head for a last withering look at the pool-hall operator, and his expression suddenly became intent.

Allie was stooped over his counter, scribbling on some surface. An innocuous thing and meaningless in itself, but a sudden thought started through Devereaux and shook him violently. He edged back over the doorway, then flung rapidly back into the pool hall.

Allie hurriedly palmed the surface he had been writing

on, and Devereaux fought it out of his hand. It was a business card. On the back of it the pool-hall operator had jotted down two names: Martie Phillips and Fred Castle.

"What about it?" Devereaux demanded grimly.

"Just made a note of those names." Allie was conquering a spasm of panic. "In case I could turn up some information for you."

"For yourself, you mean! You were going to check into those names, and see whether some blackmail angle could be worked up." Devereaux tore the card into fragments and flung them into the pool-hall operator's face. "Cough up," he commanded.

"Cough up what?"

"Two hundred and sixty dollars."

"Welshing a bet?" Allie said nastily.

"Welshing on a skunk."

"You'll have to take it back."

"One more provocation and I will." Devereaux's facial muscles quivered. "I'd start a bonfire with that two hundred and sixty dollars if I could give you the thrashing you rate."

"I'm sixty-one," Allie said, building a moral barricade between them.

"That's your damned good luck," Devereaux raged. "Now give it back!"

Allie dropped a crumpled roll of bills on the counter. "Kick my ass for trusting a copper," he said.

Devereaux pocketed the money. "Remember those two names and I'll make a career of hounding you."

"Kick my goddam ass for trusting a copper," Allie said miserably.

CHAPTER FIFTEEN

1.

The pinewood coffin with silver handles in the store window of the McBride Mortuary Parlor was carefully centered on a strip of red velvet carpeting. To one side of it stood a large onyx-marble vase filled with fresh white roses. Balanced against the vase, a white square card announced in old-style script: "No Business Solicited Until William McBride Jr.'s Return."

Devereaux stood at the door with a box of glazed thin mints under his arm, and yanked a pulley cord that rang a bell inside the funeral parlor.

Long after, the door opened. He saw a gnomelike creature with a corrugated face and eyes that seemed to thrust at him. "There'll be no business until Bill gets back," she said testily.

"I came for a social chat." Devereaux smiled. He held the box out to her. "Brought you some peppermints."

Her mouth moved as if savoring a pleasantly remembered taste, and she took the box with eager hands.

Devereaux waited stiffly. "Come in, if you're coming in," she said, then hobbled past him to lead the way to the rear quarters.

The furnishings in the single rear room were scant: two wicker chairs, one of them a rocker, with cotton-cushion seats; a single day bed; and a circular oak table with a Victorian kerosene lamp on it. There was a thick smell of incense in the room. On one wall hung a color-tinted, life-sized photo-portrait of a plump-cheeked and balding man of fifty. Beneath it, on a mantel, was a brightly burning candle modeled into a cross. The man in the photograph was William McBride, Jr., Devereaux guessed.

They sat opposite each other, and Devereaux waited until Grandma McBride had completed a flurry of movements and was finally munching toothlessly on a thin mint.

"You're a friend of Bill's?" she asked in a high, squeaky pitch.

Devereaux nodded, squirming uncomfortably. A friend of Bill's was exactly the mild deception he had planned.

"Bill's friends are always bringing me peppermints," she said contentedly.

"When's Bill coming back?" Devereaux ventured.

"Don't know. Bill never lets me know what he's about." Her eyes thrust and remained fixed like bright twin beads. "You're not jollying an old grandma now!"

"Of course not," Devereaux protested.

"People think I'm touched, expecting Bill back," she said, then laughed as if enjoying some precious and secret joke. The eyes thrust at Devereaux. "You came to chat, you said?"

"I came to repay a small debt. Twenty dollars. Bill once made me a cash loan of twenty dollars."

"I'll take it for Bill," she said avidly. She took the bill Devereaux fumbled out of his wallet and placed it under the cotton cushion of the wicker rocker.

"You're a trustworthy young man," she said in a pleased voice.

"A debt's a debt," Devereaux replied modestly. "I've, ah, had some pretty good years since leaving the old neighborhood. Made quite a lot of money. Thought I'd, ah, drop around and help a few needy old friends."

"What's your name?" she asked.

"Mike Devers."

The flesh folded until all the features were blurred. "And your mother's name?"

"Katherine. My father was Peter Devers."

"Your family's gone out of my head," she said shaking her head dolefully.

"We lived just outside the neighborhood. Over on Maujer and Humboldt."

"Oh," she said, acquitting herself of the sin of a memory lapse. "It ain't me to forget any family that ever was in the neighborhood." There was a thin crackle of laughter. "Father Dooley, mercy to him, used to speak about the unfailing memory the Lord had given me."

Her bright eyes thrust at him. "It's a Christian thing you've come to do for old friends, Mike. Father Dooley, mercy to him, would be overjoyed."

"Maybe you can help," Devereaux said. "Finding people you haven't seen for long years is a bit of a job." He cleared his throat and took the plunge. "I was over at Number 26½, looking for the Hughes family. I couldn't find hide nor hair of them."

"Hughes," she repeated with a start, and then began to rock.

"Yes, Hughes," Devereaux repeated nervously. What had the name precipitated in the elderly lady, he wondered. What walls were being erected against him?

"It would be more Christian if you gave money to the Church in memory of poor Theresa Kellams, than to go looking for the blackhearted widow Hughes."

Devereaux's pulse leaped with the unexpected cue. "This condemnation of Frankie Hughes' mother," the detective said. "It's undoubtedly justified, but I don't understand it."

"It was Constance Hughes' duty to stand with her boy, and not go running off in dark shame and self-pity." There were unusual vigor and surprising lucidity in the elderly voice. "And it was her duty to stand with the girl, Dora, and not leave the burden all to poor Theresa Kellams."

"The girl, Dora." Devereaux fumbled helplessly. "What about the girl?"

Her eyes thrust at Devereaux, then winked approvingly. "I guess there's no harm in telling an old secret." A crackling laugh sounded. "I was never one for secrets, and this one's been rankling inside these old bones since Father Dooley passed on, mercy to him."

Devereaux waited impatiently while she found a mint, held it daintily to her mouth, and munched on it.

"Dora Kellams was a wild one, with a bright red garter under her knee low enough to blind a soul, and making free with the boys." The elderly lady clucked her tongue and pointed a gnarled finger. "Carrying on in that old cellar right next door. The Lorimer Social Club, they called it."

She rocked mirthfully, as if enjoying the recollection despite her tone of disapproval.

"The boys learned a thing or two in their social club, and the girls—" She held a suggestive palm a distance away from her stomach. "Pairing them off was a job for a judge, except with Dora Kellams and Frankie Hughes. They were to be getting married, when Frankie fell in with the police."

"They didn't marry?" Devereaux inquired.

She shook her head. "Frankie went to trial and that was the end of him."

Devereaux nodded to himself. Arrest and trial had been the end of Frankie Hughes. The scalding death had been a mere formalization of a dreary truth.

"So Dora Kellams had her baby," the detective said. "They didn't marry, and Frankie's mother disavowed Dora and her condition, but Dora had her baby."

The old lady rocked and sighed. "And died having it. And soon after, poor Theresa Kellams followed Dora to the grave."

"What became of the baby?" Devereaux asked, but he knew. Jennifer Phillips stood squarely in his mind's eye.

"Spirited away." The old lady shook her head from side

to side. "Some said Theresa Kellams had given the baby to the Sisterhood. But nobody knew anything, except that when Theresa Kellams passed on, the baby was gone."

She sighed wearily, fumbled weakly for a mint, but left her hand resting limply on the candy box.

"You're tired," Devereaux said softly. "Thanks for an interesting hour."

"Let yourself out. And come for another talk." Her eyes turned up hopefully. "Bill will be back, and we'll live the old days."

2.

"I cannot permit it without official authorization," the little man said nervously. "You will have to apply to the Superintendent of Schools." He sat up, exaggeratedly erect in his chair, as if facing up to some peril whose total dimensions were yet unknown.

"I'm a detective," Devereaux said stubbornly. "Public employee, like you. And I'm asking for a mere courtesy." He placed his credentials on the desk. "You can examine my credentials."

The hands twisted nervously, then moved through the detective's papers. Finally he said, "We don't keep clerical records older than five years in this office."

"Where do you keep them?"

"I'll have to call the custodian."

"Call him," Devereaux agreed. "I'll want to check through all the graduating classes of 1921 through 1926. I'm especially interested in class pictures." He smiled. "I can do it right in the record room with the custodian chaperoning me."

There was a pause, and the burdened look deepened in the seated man's face. Waiting, Devereaux let his eyes wander over the miscellaneous details of a public-school clerical office. The scrupulously polished desk plate read: "Marcus Leeman, Assistant to the Principal." The severe umber walls held simply framed lithographs memorializing Washington's Delaware crossing, Bunker Hill, the inauguration of Abraham Lincoln, other American lore. Centered on one wall was the school banner, blue and gold. The legend "ISAAC REMSEN JUNIOR HIGH SCHOOL—P. S. 147" was lettered across it.

Devereaux leaned down, bringing his face close to the seated man. "Let's get on with it," he said insistently.

A final flickering look of battle blurred in the man's eyes. "I'll call the custodian," he said fretfully.

CHAPTER SIXTEEN

The rich promise of scandal burned vividly in the elevator operator's face. He sent the car on its upward climb with his eyes hard and urgent on Devereaux, as if trying to compel a juicy morsel of gossip. Devereaux smiled slightly. The display of his badge and the implications of a detective's unannounced call on *the* Martin Phillips had stunned and then intrigued the building manager and his lackeys.

The elevator door closed behind Devereaux, and the detective was alone in the few cubic feet of foyer space connecting the penthouse suite and the elevator. He paused before the door for an uneasy moment, and then pushed the buzzer firmly.

The remembered blustering tones called an inquiry through the closed door. Devereaux remained mute, waiting, and then pressed the buzzer imperatively. Soon the door inched open, and the first thing in the detective's vision was a small-caliber revolver pointed at waist level.

"May I come in?" Devereaux said coolly.

The revolver moved with him as the detective crossed the room and found a chair facing the terrace. He looked at Phillips curiously. The corseted illusion of compactness was gone. The flesh was fallen, as if the critic were liquifying. The sick-looking face was even paler than before; the eyes, brows, mouth looked like penciling on a calcimined parchment. Phillips was fully dressed, ready for the street, and chafing like a man whose momentum had been forced to a sudden halt. Across the room, at the foot of a gleaming grand piano, were two trim Gladstone suitcases. A fading sticker on one of them in Devereaux's view read gaily, "Bermuda, the Vacation Paradise."

"Taking a trip, huh?" Devereaux met Phillips' burning dislike solemnly. He pointed a thumb loosely. "That wouldn't be the murder gun?"

Phillips glowered resentfully, disdaining the imputation, and Devereaux continued, "A small-caliber gun killed Longo, Castle, and Latimer." He gestured at the bags. "You're packed and ready to skip."

Some moments later, after a silence, the detective observed, "How far can you get?"

Phillips sank into a chair, with the gun pointing at his feet. "I didn't murder anybody," he said drearily.

"Who did?"

The mouth opened to speak, then drew into a determined line.

"It's late in the day, Phillips," the detective said quietly. "Silence now will get you nowhere. Not with four murders to be accounted for."

The critic's mouth held unyieldingly, and Devereaux repeated, "I said *four* murders."

Phillips' jaw seemed to drop in slow-motion stages. Devereaux said, "You see, I know about the murder of Frankie Hughes by Longo in Sing Sing. In fact, there's very little I don't know." He looked at Phillips solemnly. "Martin Phillips, fifty thousand dollars a year, man of letters and a man of importance. You've come a long way from the Brooklyn street ruffian who attended Public School 147 as Carl Randau."

A deepening fear filled Phillips' face as the detective continued. "The police tracking down Frankie Hughes' confederates in that Hubbell Electrical Appliance payroll holdup and shooting found themselves wandering in circles in a hostile neighborhood of police haters. Besides, they probably relaxed in the belief that sooner or later the convicted Hughes would break down and inform on his confederates. The same logic probably influenced the judge to bait Hughes into a confession by imposing the staggered kind of sentence he did. I went to Williamsburg with the knowledge that you, Castle, Latimer, and Hughes had some common identity as a group. Knowing that gave me an advantage the police never had.

"I also had photographs of you, Castle, and Latimer. Photographs of men in their forties." Devereaux smiled faintly. "Photographically, the man of forty is the boy of eighteen. There are differences, of course. More sag to the cheeks and jowls, more roundness in the face, some baldness, crow's-feet. But the features essentially remain unchanged. A slight touching-up, and a photographer or an artist can make the photograph of the man of forty look twenty years younger in a jiffy."

Devereaux's eyes met Phillips'. "It wasn't even too much of a job going behind the man of forty and visualizing the beardless boy of fifteen. I was able to pick you, Latimer, Castle, and Frankie Hughes out of a group picture of thirty-eight in the graduating class of 1923 of the Isaac Remsen Junior High School. Except for Hughes, your names were different, and there were enough look-alikes in the flat photography of the period to puzzle me a little. But I was sure enough to be willing to make book on my identification.

"From there, I checked further, just to make doubly sure. I followed the continuing scholastic career of Carl Randau alias Martin Phillips, and Paul Boerum alias Frederick J. Castle, to the Eastern District High School. Latimer's schooling ended with Isaac Remsen, but his facial characteristics even at fifteen were so pronounced there could be no mistaking him as Terrence Dugan, just as there finally could be no mistake in my conclusive identification of you and Castle in your pictures in the high-school graduating class of 1926."

A tense pause later, Devereaux said with just a tinge of sympathy, "Big stuff, that payroll holdup, for kids of eighteen."

"It was crazy bravado," Phillips said emptily. "We were always talking about big, bold doings, as kids do. We talked of crime and vast sums of money all through our childhood. At eighteen we fertilized the seed." The critic shuddered and added huskily, "And reaped the whirlwind."

"What happened to the payroll money?"

Phillips hesitated slightly. "We split it."

"When Hughes went to jail, who got his share?"

Phillips resumed a wary silence, and Devereaux said, "I had an hour's chat with Grandma McBride." The detective eyed the critic keenly. "Hughes' share went to the care of his—daughter." He couldn't mouth the word "illegitimate."

Phillips stared, then nodded confirmation. Devereaux regarded him critically, "How did you become, ah, sole custodian of Jennifer Hughes?"

"By elimination. We'd pledged our word to Frankie that we'd care for the child as long as necessary. As it developed, Castle and Latimer had little stomach for the responsibility. I saw it through alone."

"What made you decide to pose as her father?"

Phillips flushed. "I'm not sure. As years passed, it seemed inevitable that I must. For convenience, and for appearances, too. Then, the child was growing, asking questions that were embarrassingly direct. The decision, in a sense, was compelled upon me."

"Perhaps, too, you found her a compelling child. Did that help motivate your decision?"

"I don't understand your remark," Phillips said.

"How old was she when you decided to come forward as her father?"

"Ten, I think."

"She was a beautiful child, who gave promise of growing into a beautiful young woman."

"So," Phillips said forbiddingly.

Devereaux hesitated. His mind was racing back over the mood of his first encounter with Jennifer. The girl had said little actually, submitting the mere sketch of a tyrannical overlord in her bid for his, Devereaux's, help. What had really won him to her cause had been the great unexpressed revulsion in her for Phillips.

"Your motives weren't altruistic *or* cavalier, Phillips," the detective said intensely. The same hot waves of anger he had once felt for the critic were surging through him now. "You didn't just adopt an orphaned waif, the misbegotten daughter of a man who was keeping faith with you while wasting in jail. You bought the girl as a beautiful object, as something to own and enjoy, like your sybaritic perfumes and exotic foods."

The detective watched the critic flinch. "I don't exactly know what you're about, or what classification of animal you really rate, and I'd give a hundred dollars for a clinical report on you. But this much is as obvious as your aromatic personality: you're not a man among men, and you're not a man among women, and playing father and counselor to an adolescent girl as you have is as unnatural and obscene as a dirty drawing on an outhouse wall."

Phillips was on his feet, glaring, with the gun held stiffly in front of him.

Devereaux watched the face purple and the colored veins sprout and lump over the skin. He watched the cheeks and hands tremble as if in the first warning stages of an epileptic convulsion.

It showed the detective more than the disorder of a man at bay, more than the natural hypertensions of a man whose finely spun existence was unraveling, unraveled in fact. The lunatic moment was a close gauge of Phillips. The man was a psychopath, capable of violence, capable of murder. The cold reserve that was his professional habit was a cardboard façade. A wild man lived inside the critic. A wild man precariously leashed behind the corseted front. And the leash had snapped.

The moment passed, and Phillips sank quiveringly into his seat, as if totally drained by his Jekyll-like transfiguration. The detective observed quietly, "You're easily capable of murder, Phillips. You could have murdered me a minute ago. It cost you more of an effort not to."

Devereaux shook his head. "It wasn't my gibes or taunts *or* your reaction to my plain dislike for you, or even because in a way I'm responsible for the final collapse of your barricaded world." The detective paused to organize his thinking. This man was an absorbing and complex riddle.

"You've lived all of your life with a hand on the trigger, keeping the outside world at a distance but within target range. Read the critical stuff you write. Every word a sniper's bullet. Never a word of praise for the other fellow, the ordinary Joe. You see people around as sitting ducks, and you see yourself as some godlike Olympian, able to snuff out their lives and hopes at will. That's why you live in this sky tower, way up over the heads of people, looking down on the mob, the sitting ducks you hate. And that's why you come apart at the seams and go berserk when someone dares to touch you."

Phillips said, "Shut up, dammit. Shut up."

The detective went on grimly. "A crime you'd gotten away with long ago when one of your crowd was nervy and loyal enough to take a solitary rap without squealing suddenly came alive all over again. An incident of your past suddenly dared touch you. People whom you despised suddenly broke into your sky tower, to corner you and touch you. Your one-time confederates, Hughes, Castle, Latimer. The crooked ex-insurance operative, Buloff. The tool, Longo. Me, a detective who popped up from nowhere with an infuriating curiosity about you. A lot of people suddenly crowding you. A lot of people telling you that while they lived, you couldn't ever again live alone in your sky tower." Devereaux nodded to himself, as if accepting his own outline. "A lot of people, Phillips. A lot of people to kill!"

A long while later, Phillips said tonelessly, "I didn't murder anybody."

"Who did?"

A deep breath sounded in his chest, and Phillips said, "Buloff. He killed Longo, Castle, and Latimer."

Devereaux cocked an eyebrow and said nothing. Phillips looked blindly at the gun pointing in his lap. "Buloff tried to kill me, too. I thought it was he when you rang my bell."

"When did Buloff try to kill you?"

"Last night, at three A.M., in the Studor Garage. I'd driven my car into the lower level, to park it for the night. Buloff was there, waiting in ambush. I sensed his presence, probably because I'd been expecting him to make an attempt on me."

"And?" the detective prompted.

"He came out of the shadows, and stood at the door of my car. I remained in the car, crouched to the floor, locked in and trapped. Then I honked my horn and created a mad din." A ghostly smile played on the critic's mouth. "He fired through the plate glass twice, and fled. The thick plate glass deflected the bullets."

"Did the horn and shots attract anyone?"

"Just the night attendant. I gave him a hundred dollars to keep mum about the incident and dispose of the shattered plate glass." The smile played faintly again. "I told him it was a jealous husband, and that I wanted no scandal."

"I'll check the story," Devereaux said. "And if it's true, a night attendant is going to jail for failure to report an attempted murder to the police."

The critic shrugged. "Check it and be damned."

"Now that you're getting it off your chest," Devereaux said, "can I ask some direct questions?"

The critic shook his head slightly, then shrugged, "All right. Ask them."

"What made the elaborate plot for killing Frankie Hughes in Sing Sing so necessary?"

"Hughes had served notice that he was going to confess, implicate Latimer, Castle, and me, when brought back before the court."

"How did Hughes serve notice of his intention?"

"In a letter smuggled out and mailed by a freed convict."

"Mailed to whom?"

Phillips hesitated, and the detective prompted, "To Mrs. Cora Jennings, was it? I know all about Mrs. Jennings."

"Yes, to Mrs. Jennings."

"What exactly was Mrs. Jennings' role in this whole affair?"

"A revolting busybody," Phillips said with flashing irritation. "The hideous myth of the great slobbering maternal heart come true."

Devereaux smiled. "Besides getting under your skin, exactly what did she do?"

"When Dora Kellams died, the baby's grandmother had left Jennifer with Mrs. Jennings, an old acquaintance. Mrs. Jennings ran a nursery and boardinghouse up near White Plains. Later, with the grandmother's death, Mrs. Jennings insisted that the baby be allowed to stay on in her care. We wanted to place the child somewhere else, but Mrs. Jennings had her way."

"She'd tumbled to the story?"

"To part of it. She knew who Jennifer's father was, about Frankie Hughes being in Sing Sing. Just that. She'd gotten the hysterical Theresa Kellams to blab that much. She didn't know about me or the others. She didn't know, but she probably guessed the truth, guessed that our interest was more than just discreet friendship for an unfortunate comrade in prison." Phillips made a face. "Anyhow, she got in touch with Hughes, gave him carefully worded bulletins on the baby's progress regularly, and got Hughes to instruct us to pay liberally for the child's support. She won Hughes' confidence, and through the years, right to the end, they kept up a lively correspondence."

"How were you able to transfer the child, and take over custody later?"

"With Hughes' consent." Phillips flushed. "I had prospered and become somebody important, somebody who could give the girl advantages. Hughes prevailed upon Mrs. Jennings to go along with my plans." The critic shuddered. "In taking over management of the child, I also took over the onus of Mrs. Jennings. She haunted and hounded me through the years, watching the results of my stewardship over the girl, watching the girl's progress, and reporting to Hughes."

Devereaux nodded. Plainly, the idea of Phillips' control over the nurture and growth of Jennifer had affronted Mrs. Jennings, and through her, ultimately, the putative father. How much of this anger and disillusionment had influenced Hughes' decision to break his silence, Devereaux wondered. He framed his next question, and then discarded it. Foolhardy, baiting Phillips; not while the man was so obligingly talkative.

"It was that correspondence between Hughes and Mrs. Jennings that sent Longo to her room at the Hotel Orleans."

Phillips nodded. "She suspected Hughes' death wasn't accidental, as it seemed to be. She came here and made a scene, accusing me."

A thought held Devereaux. "Then Longo didn't just go to her room for that correspondence. He went there to kill her, but her heart seizure made murder superfluous."

Phillips kept silent, and the detective said, "Whose idea was it, killing Hughes in jail before he got to talking?"

"Buloff's. He plotted it, and forced the rest of us to go

along with him. Longo was his man. Buloff promised him a twenty-thousand-dollar fee for the job, and promised to maneuver Longo into an early parole."

"Just when did Buloff enter the picture?"

"A few years after Hughes' sentence. He found out about us, exactly how I don't know, and gave us the choice of paying blackmail or facing arrest." Phillips' face darkened. "We paid."

"How much?"

"We gave him the lion's share of the stolen money. Subsequently, as all of us prospered, Castle, Latimer and myself, Buloff made further demands, exorbitant demands. In effect, he declared himself a lifetime partnership in our successes and fortunes."

"He really cut himself a big piece of pie, huh?"

Phillips nodded miserably, and his voice wrenched a little. "And we cut ourselves a piece of that hell Buloff gibbers about when we threw in with him to save ourselves. Buloff is a complete madman."

Devereaux grinned. "I've seen the hell he owns and operates at close hand."

"He never let up on us." Now there was a violent note of outrage. "More than just taking our money, he took a sadistic pleasure in torturing us. We were compelled to visit his Mission and make platform speeches about sin and purgatory to bums and inebriates, reading from notes Buloff had prepared for us." Phillips' face flamed with the recollection. "Buloff would introduce us as men who were successful but damned, glittering object lessons for the forgathered, and then sit on the dais enjoying what we were forced to say, with his eyes mocking us as we spoke. Wherever we'd be, myself, Latimer, Castle, a sudden peremptory telegram would order us to a command visit. Invariably it was Easter, Christmas, or some other holiday. Once we were compelled to spend a Thanksgiving weekend there. We had to submit our clothes to fumigation, eat the swill his cook prepared, and sleep in vermin-infested beds. He even forced Latimer to serve on his so-called board of directors."

Devereaux repressed a desire to laugh. "Why did you obey? And the others, why did they?"

"We were afraid of Buloff. Afraid of what he might do."

"But he was in as deeply as any of you."

Phillips shook his head. "We found little security in the knowledge. The man was unpredictable, mentally unbalanced. We even thought he might expose us all just to see us writhe, perhaps even to enjoy some masochistic moment arrest might offer him." The critic paused, then added seriously, "The man makes a fetish of self-denial, self-castigation. He really believes in the gibberish he spews about Hell and suffering in life."

Devereaux said, "If so, how does that jibe with your charge that he did the murders? Would a man making a creed of self-denial and self-abasement take such a desperate and immoral way of saving himself?"

Phillips said uncertainly, "A masochist could. By increasing his guilt, he increased his pain and his own enjoyment of pain. His personal hell became something more acute, and therefore he got a bigger kick out of it." He shrugged. "I don't know. I don't pretend to understand Buloff. The man's a chameleon, impossible to fathom."

"Maybe he's just a fakir," Devereaux suggested. "Maybe he sold you all on his, ah, uniqueness just to keep you in line while he bled you at will. If you'd believed him a normal scoundrel, just a little eccentric maybe, you could have shut off tribute any time you chose to, since Buloff couldn't expose any of you without exposing himself, too."

Phillips seemed to be considering it. "It's an idea," he said indifferently, as if the question were now purely academic.

"Buloff has a string of aliases, and something of a record. As an insurance detective, he did a pretty slick job where the police failed dismally. He broke the case, double-crossed the company, grabbed the spoils, and put the bite on your crowd from then on in a pretty ingenious way. When threatened with exposure, he found a way of murdering a man who was safely behind bars. None of these things suggest a mentally unbalanced fanatic. All of these things suggest a criminal with a cold, logical mind and a genius for self-preservation."

"Then it was all a masquerade with Buloff," Phillips said. "What's the difference now?"

Devereaux regarded him quizzically. "Did you trail me to Ossining one night?"

Phillips shook his head.

"Did we have an unexpected encounter in the Attic Circus the morning Latimer was found dead?"

Phillips shook his head firmly.

"Your servant, Sato, where is he?"

"I dismissed him from my employ."

"And the girl, where is she?"

"I don't know."

"When did you see her last?"

"Early this morning." Phillips looked at the detective curiously. "What's your interest in Jennifer?"

Devereaux ignored the query. "You insist that beyond involuntary complicity in the murder of Hughes, you are innocent of the other killings?"

Phillips nodded. "I didn't kill Longo or Castle or Latimer," he supplemented huskily.

"It won't make too much difference in how you fare in court," the detective said. "Accessory to the murder of Frankie Hughes, plus complicity in the shooting of that Electrical Company bank messenger, is enough to get you life imprisonment at the very least." He thrust his arm out, palm up. "I'll take your gun now."

Phillips said, "No." The reckless tensions were back in him.

"Careful," Devereaux said uneasily. The gun was pointing at his middle. "A muscular spasm in your hands, and the gun might go off."

"Then don't try to stop me," Phillips warned.

"Phillips, you're crazy. The game's up, and just playing hard to catch will get you nothing but a lot of fatigue. Leave here, and you'll have every cop in town, and the forty-eight states around, looking for you." Devereaux's tone sharpened, "Play fugitive, even for one day, and it's just that much more press copy, that much more tabloid scandal, another published picture of Jennifer, another hour of crucifixion for her. Dammit, for the girl's sake, for the final consideration you owe her, surrender quietly, now, here to me, and give me a chance to see if I can keep her in the background, keep her out of it as much as possible. The girl's got a future to live!"

Phillips said softly, "This concern I've sensed before, this really extraordinary concern for the girl!"

Devereaux set his teeth. "I'll take your gun."

Phillips' gun hand thrust forward rigidly. "Turn around and walk toward that closet across the room." His voice quickened. "Walk."

Devereaux approached the closet slowly.

"Open the door," Phillips ordered.

"Look," the detective said grimly, holding the closet door ajar. "I've taken quite a shellacking from a lot of punks. I've had a stretch in the hospital. Slug me, and I give you my solemn word that the next time we meet—"

His teeth were a guillotine knife slicing downward to cut off his speech, as an abyss opened to receive him.

CHAPTER SEVENTEEN

1.

He rested on one knee, low to the floor, and let his energies revive. His head was throbbing, and there was cotton batting over his eardrums that insulated him against sound.

Bz-zzz. The sound was lost to him.

He climbed a notch higher, rested again, and forced his hearing. Bz-zzz, the sound came again. He strained to identify it.

It was a door buzzer.

He felt along the walls of the narrow closet, and found the door. He tested it, and again, then rattled the doorknob furiously.

The sound outside the chamber stopped, and Devereaux mustered his strength into a single flinging push.

The closet door held. He flung himself again, then sagged against a wall gasping for breath.

There was a new sound outside—a shout, reverberating in a vast echo chamber. He rattled the doorknob feverishly, and banged with a fist.

Soon a key turned in the lock and the door jerked open.

The picture formed slowly before him. He saw the gun first, then the face.

It was Captain Anders.

"Hello." Devereaux grinned foolishly.

"Where's Phillips?" Anders rasped.

"Powdered." Devereaux fell into a chair. "What brought *you?*"

"Elevator starter phoned headquarters. All puzzled and anxious. Said a detective came up here and never came down again." Anders made a clucking sound in his mouth. "We were to leave Phillips to you," he said ironically. "Solowey made a big point of that yesterday."

"Sorry," Devereaux said. "He got the drop on me, and was worked up enough to plug me."

Anders looked at him searchingly. "Why does Phillips rate special and exclusive handling?"

"He doesn't. Not any more."

"You've got a case on his daughter, huh?"

"She isn't his daughter."

"Okay, his so-called daughter. Quit being evasive," Anders said irritably. "All wrapped up and sentimental, and anxious to handle a case with kid gloves! Acting like a public-relations man, instead of a cop!" He said it as if it were very incomprehensible to him. "Kid gloves! That's a wrinkle in you I never saw before. Not ever, in twenty years."

"Shut up, Anders."

"Sure. Throw the kid gloves into the garbage can, and I'll shut up. Don't, and I'll yell you right into the mayor's office." He looked demandingly at Devereaux. "Now, how do we solve a murder case? A mass murder case, I mean."

"Send an alarm out for Phillips."

"I already did. Was it Phillips?"

"He swears he didn't. Swears it was Maxim Buloff."

"Buloff is hard to catch. The alarm's been out since Solowey fed me that piecemeal story you sent him downtown with, but no trace of Buloff." Anders rubbed his chin. "Who do you think the killer is?"

"Buloff, probably. If Phillips wasn't putting a show on for me. But I'm not going out on a limb." Devereaux started for the door. "Coming?"

Anders brushed past him. "Going. You stay. Solowey's on his way over with your apple-cheeked charmer." He answered the question forming on Devereaux's mouth. "I called Solowey, to check on whether it was you the elevator starter was all worked up over." He shook his head reprovingly, then looked into Devereaux's face defiantly. "Give me one reason why I can't arrest the lady as a material witness."

Devereaux wet his lips. "You know the one reason," he said quietly. "Nothing will be withheld, I promise you. The whole story, all of it, right down to the last comma, will go down on the blotter."

They stood eye to eye and Devereaux felt himself flush. "Okay," Anders said doubtfully. "Okay," he repeated, satisfied, and opened the door.

At the door he stopped suddenly. "You're not planning to marry her!" Anders said.

"Guess I am," Devereaux said softly. "I am," he repeated, sure of it.

Anders' whistle of surprise seemed to hang in the air long after the door had closed behind him.

2.

It seemed hours later when Solowey came in with his arm locked in Jennifer's.

Devereaux smiled fondly at the picture they made. A fat Buddha and a misty-eyed nymph.

Solowey moved self-effacingly to a side, like a supernumerary yielding the center of the stage to the stars.

They stood apart for a moment, then moved in accord. Her arms crept around his neck.

"Tears," Devereaux chided lumpily. "What for?"

"You might have been killed," she wept softly.

"Somebody's been playing on your imagination, kid." He looked across to Solowey accusingly. "Some old fossil's been trying to make a dull trade sound like Dick Tracy."

"A libelous guess," Solowey said wryly. "And shame on

you, Devereaux." He moved toward the pair. "She knows the whole story. About who she is, about Phillips and the others." His voice sank to a barely audible register. "About her father, her real father."

Devereaux looked at her questioningly. "Early this morning," she said. "Phillips came home at four o'clock and knocked on my door. He was shaken, as if he had been through a horrible ordeal. He said he wanted to talk. He sat on the edge of my bed and talked, right through the dawn until forenoon."

Devereaux spoke to Solowey. "Buloff tried to kill him in the Studor Garage at three A.M." He turned to Jennifer solicitously. "Where did you go when you left here?"

"To the park. I sat, I don't know how long. There was so much to think about, to think over." Her mouth trembled. "My mother, the tragedy of it. And my father, murdered in prison."

Devereaux took her hand and led her to a chair. "He gave you the whole dose at once, huh?" His voice grated. "He had to get it off his conscience, even if it killed *you*."

Solowey sought a share in the indignation. "She arrived at my office an hour ago, still suffering from shock, and looking for you."

"I tried to find you for hours." Her face turned up to Devereaux's. "I rang your bell over and over."

"I was here, holding a séance with Phillips practically since noon." Devereaux touched his head tenderly and motioned to the closet. "I also took quite a long nap in there."

Solowey's fingers felt along Devereaux's skull gently. "You have an extraordinary immunity to brain concussion. Just a lump, no bigger than a chestnut. You have a head of iron."

Devereaux grinned humorlessly. "When times get rough, I'll stick my head through a canvas flap and let circus patrons throw baseballs at it." He looked down on Jennifer and watched her hands twine and untwine.

"Jumpy, huh?" Devereaux said.

"Johnny, I want to pack and leave here forever. That's why I came."

"Sure," Devereaux agreed heartily. "Pack up and get. That's the ticket." He cupped his hand under her chin and cleared his throat noisily. "Got any plans?"

"No." Her eyes met his with just a trace of coquetry. "No plans, Johnny."

He looked at her for an eternal moment, unable to say it. "A month at an inn will do wonders for you. By then things will have simmered down."

She squeezed his hand gratefully.

"Got any idea where Phillips might have bolted to?" Devereaux inquired, pushing the impulse to propose further into the future.

She shook her head blankly.

"No sanctuary, no favorite retreat?"

Her face drew in concentration, and then went vague. "Perhaps Martha's Vineyard, or Dennis on the Cape. He spent many weekends there over the years."

"No hint to you about what he might do, in all that talking he did? No slip of the tongue?"

She shook her head positively. "I had no idea he planned to run away."

Solowey broke in. "He'll be in custody within twenty-four hours, along with Buloff." The shoulders hunched expressively. "What chance do either of them have?" He beamed at Devereaux. "You did a magnificent job, Devereaux. I am still astonished over your exploits of yesterday in Williamsburg. For ingenuity in research and interrogation, it ranks with the best detective jobs in my knowledge."

Devereaux stuck modest fingers in his ears, and Solowey continued, "But for you now, the case is finished. Your work is done." He bent down and patted the backs of Jennifer's hands. "You have but to concern yourself with this lovely lady."

"Finished?" Devereaux echoed restlessly. "We've just got a story, and two fugitive suspects."

"A few harried hours, and they'll be caught. Whether it was Buloff or Phillips, the exact degree of guilt of each of them is of small importance, a mere postscript to the real story." Solowey looked significantly at Devereaux. "It would be better if you let Captain Anders write that postscript, my good Devereaux. A shallow triumph, but it would do much to assuage ruffled tempers, and perhaps acquit you of some, ah, anarchy in procedure I have heard much grumbling about."

The corners of his mouth dropped, and Devereaux shrugged, accepting the injunction. "Start packing."

Solowey went to the door. "That is an oblique way of saying: Solowey, start going." A chuckle ran through his ponderous frame. "In my time on this earth, I have read much of the literature of romance. I have been diverted by the imaginative ways in which authors, the classical and popular both, contrive to have the swain meet his lady. But you, Devereaux, have written a new and flaming chapter." He bowed gallantly toward the reddening Devereaux. "Its baptism in fire is a sure guarantee that your romance will endure where others wither."

"How corny can you get, Mr. Solowey!" Devereaux raised a vase threateningly. "Stick a final bill for services rendered in the mail, Cupid."

"Don't look for it." Solowey's eyes twinkled. "I cannot see an aged, retired detective ending up on the dole, so I decided to forgive your last bill. Perhaps I can persuade the tax collector that it was an operational loss for the Solowey Agency."

Devereaux grinned gratefully, and Solowey raised an admonishing hand. "On condition that you and your lady sit as my guests at a victory dinner." He read his pocket watch, and squinted across the room at a Dresden porcelain clock teeming with cherubs and rosebuds. "It is three-thirty now. Let us say six-thirty, at the Café Frontenac?"

"It's a deal," Devereaux agreed.

Solowey departed.

CHAPTER EIGHTEEN

1.

Devereaux dragged a steamer trunk out of a closet, opened it, then followed the girl dutifully while she moved about the room, emptying drawers of neatly folded stockings, lingerie, garments, trinkets, the miscellaneous welter of items that are the ordinary and bizarre accumulations of living and use.

There was a melancholy in her that firmly and inexorably excluded him, as all pain must slight those who would share in it vicariously. There were moments when the melancholy plunged into morbidness, as the litter and memorabilia taken from the bureau drawers, the night stand, the jewel chest, and set in a pile, subtly became a towering monument to a haunted past.

"I was fifteen," she said, holding up a group picture of schoolgirls in hiking togs.

Devereaux looked into her face, pressing to unite with the memory. But her face was cold and her eyes uninviting as she dropped the photograph into the trunk and hurried about her next chore. She was deep within herself, alone, and jealous of her solitude.

"Yell, if you need me," Devereaux said, and wandered off. He was spent, to his limits. The burdening weight of the girl's mood was a last tax he couldn't absorb.

The detective found the wine decanter, poured himself a sherry, drifted to the terrace with the glass in his hand, and sank into a chair.

TAKE YOUR FORD BACK HOME, the sign read a half mile away across the city rooftops. Devereaux sipped his drink, and a hypnotic calm settled over him. Long ago, a long century ago, he had sat in this same chair with both the sign and Phillips eating berries in his vision. He watched a lone pigeon soar and plummet somewhere into the maze of the city. His lids nodded, and he set the wine glass on the stone floor, then slumped deeper into his seat.

The City around was throbbing in his ears, speaking to him in the special and secret dialect understood only by those who understood her. *See that coal barge being towed down the East River. Four ragged boys once stood on the opposite shore and threw defiant pebbles into the river. Four boys, Latimer, Castle, Phillips, and Hughes. Dugan, Boerum, Randau, and Hughes. A pebble into the river, a desperate shout for help. A pebble sending endless waves rippling into tomorrow, to meet with the roar of tomorrow's storms. A shout for help that wrote murder into blaring headlines.*

Devereaux's fingers dropped loosely over the side of his chair to coil around the rim of his wine glass.

Dugan, Boerum, Randau, and Hughes. Hughes, who traveled just a few miles up the river. Don't dislike him, Devereaux. He gave you a bride. A Williamsburg ruffian left a bride on the doorstep of your Chicago tenement more than twenty years ago. And the others, the three who crossed the river, who took the winding road to tomorrow because a fourth stood sacrificially in the prisoners' dock. Don't hate them, Devereaux. In bitterness they found strength. Out of resentment they forged weapons that drove them beyond the stinging memory of birth. Castle did it with pamphlets, Phillips with words, Latimer with his fists. You can't hate them, Devereaux, not with understanding. Pity them. See how the winding road that led them into tomorrow only led them back to yesterday.

Devereaux's eyes opened, widening into circles. TAKE YOUR FORD BACK HOME, the sign read.

Take your moral sermon back home, Solowey, the detective whispered to himself. I've been talking inside my head again, in your words.

A look of quiet amusement flickered in his face. The fat Buddha had furnished a corner of his, Devereaux's, brain, and was sprawling there in great, philosophical amiability, editing and interpreting the currents of his host's thinking.

I'll evict you, Devereaux promised. Toss you into the cold on your oversize bottom. But the fat Buddha was complacently waving a long-term lease.

The telephone's ringing emptied into the great hum around him. It had rung a fifth time when Devereaux lifted the receiver.

"Hello?"

It was Solowey, as if magically summoned by his thinking.

It was an unwontedly shrill Solowey, burbling an incomprehensible jargon.

"Say it again. One word at a time."

Solowey retold his tidings. Devereaux could hear the breath whistling, feel the heaving excitement in Solowey's ponderous frame course through the telephone.

Devereaux hung up slowly, remained still for a brooding moment, then stirred to Jennifer standing beside him.

"What is it, Johnny?" she exclaimed, reading his expression.

"Buloff killed Phillips, emptied a gun into him less than an hour ago." The detective assembled what he'd heard into a bulletin. "Buloff trailed him in a rented car to a cottage just a mile out of New City, up in Rockland County. Cottage was called Bolo Rest, a summer place owned by Phillips, according to the Rockland State Troopers."

The detective tapped a cigarette against a palm. "The

police will never get to write that postscript Solowey magnanimously granted them. The question of who done it, Buloff or Phillips, is a blank line on the police blotter only guesswork can fill in now."

Her face was wan and white as it strained at him questioningly. "Buloff tried to shoot his way through a roadblock on Route 9W. The State Troopers won hands down." Devereaux stopped fretfully. The sudden explosive climax left many things unresolved. It was rowdy, disorderly—a finality with everything up in the air. It mocked his innate sense of order, his reverence for patterns into which every least detail fell into place. Somehow, he felt that he had been cheated.

"There's just about enough left of Buloff for purposes of identification," Devereaux said dismally.

A silence lengthened oppressively, until it was a suspended weight that must crash. Jennifer stared at the detective dumbly, her face drawn and begging for creature reassurance. Devereaux saw her, then lost her, as his thoughts were caught in a maelstrom of details that were suddenly flooding his consciousness.

"Funny," he said aloud, snatching a piece of driftwood out of the churning mass. "Funny that with the jig up, Buloff still had to track Phillips down and kill him. Only a complete madman would need to." His lips pursed. "Phillips was probably right in his analysis of Buloff after all.

"Unless," Devereaux reflected aloud a moment later, "Buloff saw Phillips as the cause of his jeopardy and his downfall, and had to retaliate personally as a last gesture of revenge."

The reflection keyed another idea. "In that case," Devereaux said excitedly, "Buloff didn't murder Latimer, Longo, and Castle. Phillips did the murders, and Buloff knew it, as Buloff must know it!"

The detective let it elaborate in his mind. "With the first threat of police inquiry, Phillips decided to save himself by murdering everyone else involved with him. It was a large order, but Phillips' whole life was at stake. And murder as an out wouldn't deter him, since he was already accessory to two murders. The murder that convicted your father, and the murder of your father by the hireling, Longo."

Devereaux shook his head, dissatisfied, and lapsed back into silence. Another piece of driftwood was thrusting at him from the boiling mass.

"Johnny," the girl began, then started anxiously as his eyes swept her face.

A flush started in the center of her cheeks and spread to her eyes, chin, and ears. Devereaux was studying her critically from some cold corner of his brain.

"Johnny, what's wrong?"

"The Bolo Rest," Devereaux said icily, with his eyes hard and clear as if a blindfold had suddenly dropped. "Buloff trailed Phillips to a summer cottage called the Bolo Rest. The State Troopers reported the cottage was owned by Phillips. That he summered there."

It seemed to mean nothing to her. Her face showed her puzzling it out.

"The Bolo Rest," Devereaux said harshly. "When you came in with Solowey, I asked you whether Phillips had a sanctuary or a retreat somewhere he could run to if he wanted to hide."

Her mouth trembled forming a reply. "Don't waste your breath lying," the detective said. "You knew about the place. It was as familiar to you as anything in your life."

Devereaux walked a few paces, then back again. "In lying earlier, you set your own trap. Solowey has a father-and-daughter magazine picture of you and Phillips in a New City Country Club horse show." The detective's mouth worked. "The association came over me a little late. I couldn't see the woods. I was occupied with looking at you!"

"Johnny, please!"

Devereaux let an emotion course through him and run out of him. When he felt empty and drained and mechanical, he said, "You wanted Phillips to escape long enough for Buloff to track him down?"

Silence.

"Answer the question!"

"Yes."

"Why?"

"I don't know." She looked away. "I wanted him dead, for what he'd done."

"And Buloff. Did you want him dead for what he'd done?"

Silence.

"Look at me and answer the question!"

She turned back, but her eyes were lowered. "Yes."

"And the others," Devereaux said slowly, frightened at the direction he was inexorably moving in. "Longo, Castle, Latimer. Did you want them dead for what they'd done?"

Devereaux wet his lips, waiting for her reply. He had an impulse to close his ears, pull a switch and stop the machinery of his mind.

"I wanted them dead for what they'd done," she said in the grotesque refrain that had become the motive of the interrogation.

"For what they'd done," Devereaux echoed nonsensically. There were gargoyles in his head doing an idiotic, whirling dance to the refrain *I want them dead for what they'd done.*

"They murdered my father," he heard her say from some distant dreamlike void. Her voice was different. The young-girl accent was gone. It was a voice with a new, harsh quality. It was the voice of fever.

"A man you never knew." Devereaux sought to regain his balance. She was facing him now, her eyes boring into him steadily, as if through some subtle transposition she was now the inquisitor.

"How could you feel vengeful, or hate? You never saw your father or knew him."

"I did know him," she said starkly. "I knew him and loved him."

It was baffling; it made no sense to him. It was a rebuttal done sheerly for opportunity by a wily contestant engaged in a test of power with him. This girl, a stranger to her own history until it reared from ambush to overwhelm her, now insisted otherwise. She was saying that her history had been hers, living inside her, festering, to become motive to her crimes of revenge.

"You never saw your father or knew him," Devereaux repeated, but now unsurely. The agony in her face was a live thing, impossible to simulate.

But she had once simulated the simple innocence of a child, the detective told himself. Her pose had been the web he had crept into. The web and the blindfold.

"I knew my father, Johnny," she said, and Devereaux listened. She was speaking with an odd, jerking rhythm, as if fighting for breath. "Since my sixteenth birthday, I knew him as closely as I could. Better than I knew anyone else in the world. I visited him, often, posing as a niece. We talked, a vast world of talk. About ethics, religion, sports, the dance, science. He was brilliant. Self-educated, but brilliant. A man of great gifts. A man with love and deep sincerity. In prison, he had read more than two thousand books. He wanted to write someday, he said. He burned to justify himself, acquit himself in the eyes of the world through some great work. We corresponded through Mrs. Jennings. His letters were magnificent. You should read his letters, Johnny!"

She had stopped for tears, but the tears didn't come. "His letters were thirty, fifty pages long. One letter that came a month before he was murdered was ninety-six pages long. Wonderful, wonderful letters. Beautifully phrased, rich in thought. And full of hope, not despair, Johnny! Not the natural despair of a mature and wise man shut away because of a single folly of youth, but full of hope. Full of hope for man, faith in his future and the future of the world."

Her face shone with fierce pride. "I took his letters, more

than two hundred of them, to a famous editor. I didn't reveal my father's identity. I just submitted the letters. The editor was impressed with my father, with his work. He wanted to publish them!"

Devereaux stared at her heated face numbly, his strength sapped by the intensity of her fire. He had the feeling of having been overpowered; his agreement with the virtue of her motive was a condition of surrender.

"What made your father decide to go before the court and tell the truth?"

"My unhappiness." Her eyes glinted. "My father was a man who could endure hell for the sake of someone else. Think of his decision to live all of his life in jail, so that others might have a chance at freedom, a chance at life. Think of the kind of man he had to be!"

Devereaux nodded mechanically, compelled. "It was my unhappiness that changed his mind, but not at once. I pleaded with him for years. I told him I needed him, and he weighed my need against the needs of the others. In the end it was Phillips that decided him. My father began to understand Phillips' deranged and possessive mania for me. He began to worry about it until he couldn't eat, read, think. My father came to know that Phillips could do no less than destroy me."

She looked at Devereaux expectantly, and he nodded. A sybarite and homosexual holding chattel title to the future of a young girl. The unnaturalness had worried him, too. He himself had felt a father's anger.

"My father made his decision," she continued, "and it made him happy. We talked over our plans. He'd make a clean breast of everything, and his sentence would be reduced. His book would be published, and I'd go to the Governor on my knees. He'd win a pardon, he had to win a pardon!" Her eyes dimmed, but the tears didn't come. "We'd live together, and I'd be his housekeeper and typist. I'd help him redeem the lost years. And he'd help me."

"Too bad it didn't happen like that," Devereaux heard himself saying.

"They murdered him," she said, and her face was deathly white. "I knew his death wasn't accidental. I watched Phillips; I saw his nervousness. I knew that somehow he, along with others, had managed to murder my father.

"They murdered him," she repeated. "For months, awake, in my nightmares, all I could see was my father scalded to death just as he'd reached the threshold of a brave, new future. For months the burns were all over me, too. I'd sleep, and a sudden fire on my chest and arms and back would start me screaming. And all I could think of was revenge. All I could think of was how to discover the identity of the others involved with Phillips."

"You didn't know Castle, Latimer, and Buloff?" Devereaux asked.

She shook her head. "My father told me the story, but he stubbornly refused to identify the others by name. He had that kind of loyalty. I just knew that Phillips and nameless others were the principals."

"So you came to me," Devereaux said.

She looked at him as if wanting desperately to deny it, then turned away slightly.

"You came to me," Devereaux repeated bitterly. "I was to be your finger man."

She faced him again, with her fingers involuntarily at her lips, shushing him.

"I was your finger man," the detective said. "Each time I turned up a new principal, you killed him. Longo, Castle, Latimer." He laughed. "I played dupe, accessory before the fact of murder. Guns went off, but a gramophone playing *Lohengrin's Wedding March* in my head drowned out all the other noises." The laugh rattled deeper. "Each time I looked into your sweet, saintly young face, I put on another blindfold."

She was before him impulsively, denying it with her arms

181

looped around his neck. Devereaux looked at her; his arms ached to press her closely to him. This was real, his senses whispered. This girl with the beautiful form and luxuriant hair standing close was real; her guilt, though real, meant less, much less than her closeness.

He pushed her away. "You hoped Buloff and Phillips, each suspecting the other, would exterminate each other," he said. "Or that the survivor would attempt escape, resist capture, and be killed, just as it happened.

"You hoped for such an outcome," Devereaux said. "Your method had the shrewd stamp of a highly qualified murderess, not the hit-or-miss desperation of a hysterical girl. And split-second timing, as if you were born to the murder game! You shot Longo in broad daylight along a crowded waterfront. An hour later, you were right behind me driving to Summit. You were able to shoot Castle while I lay unconscious and get away before the police arrived. Yesterday, with the Attic Circus closed to the public, you were able to get in and murder Latimer, then vanish into thin air in a matter of minutes."

She was shaking her head wildly, begging him to stop. The detective went on. "It was no good killing Phillips while Buloff was on the loose, out of your reach. Buloff, alive and captured, might be able to prove he couldn't have done all the murders. An alibi, maybe, accounting for his time during one of the murders. That would leave you exposed to suspicion by sheer elimination. Suspicion must fall on you sooner or later."

She was wilting, as if she would melt to the ground. "Mass slaughter," Devereaux continued in the tone of a man assaulting his own credulities. "Crimes that compare with anything on the books in my twenty years on the force. And not a twinge of conscience in you that I can discern. Just a justified look, as if murder was a deed of the highest honor! You were even packing to go off scot free, letting me wish you godspeed with adoring eyes. Letting me play the jackass right to the end!"

Devereaux's mouth screwed into an ugly cartoon of self-contempt. "Finger man and jackass!"

"I'm sorry, Johnny," she said in a tone that was little more than a breath. "I didn't mean to hurt your self-respect. It just happened—like that. I couldn't help it." Her eyes were wide and sad. "Help me, Johnny."

"Help you take that trip. Keep your guilt between you, me, and the lamppost," Devereaux said bitterly. "A perfect way out for you, huh? A caress, some moon talk at an old idiot, and murder goes off on a honeymoon to the Caribbean." He seized her arm roughly. "Work on me, kid. I'm kiss hungry, crazy in love with you. Just one kiss and three little words, and my twenty years of being a cop will blow up in smoke."

His fingers tore into her arm. "Come on, work on me. Tell me you're really gone on me. Coax me to give it up, call quits, develop amnesia, the way you did yesterday! Get busy, but quick. It's worth every ounce of sex appeal you can throw into it. A fellow who's played finger man and jackass won't mind playing fall guy!"

"I was gone on you," she said in a sick, dead voice. "And the way things are it's impossible, I know." The sob caught in her throat. "But stand with me. Please. See me through. I'm frightened."

Devereaux turned away. Some moments later, he spoke into the room, with his back to her.

"You're under arrest."

He heard her sob. "Not you, Johnny. I couldn't stand being arrested by you."

He accepted the idea implicitly, grateful for it. She couldn't be his prisoner, as he couldn't be her jailer. Some measure of her guilt was his. He had charted her course, placed the pins in the battle map for her to follow.

He went to the door, speaking as he walked. "I'll send up an arresting officer."

In the elevator going down, he thought of nothing.

2.

The word "Frontenac" was spelled out across the upper pocket on the waiter's white jacket.

Devereaux spelled the word out methodically, then over again, following it hungrily with his eyes as the waiter bustled through the room.

"Sixteen stories to the ground," Solowey was saying. "She landed on a spiked iron railing in the yard. Crucified."

Solowey sought Devereaux's eyes unsuccessfully. "I wanted to hurry over," he said miserably. "The minute I related Rockland County with that newspaper photograph of the girl and Phillips in my files, I wanted to hurry over." His eyes followed Devereaux's stare. "I knew it would hit you like a delayed reaction, just as it did me, and at about the same time. I wanted to be there, for her sake, when you realized it was she who had done the murders."

Devereaux lost the waiter and the word. "For *her* sake, Devereaux," Solowey said. "I knew what a shock you were in for, but I wanted to be there for her sake only. I knew she would need your help. I knew she would need every tenderness and reassurance, even in a hopeless situation."

Solowey found Devereaux's eyes and held them intensely. "I was afraid you could give her nothing." His voice shook a little. "I was afraid you would turn her away, let your wounded ego interfere. I was afraid you would turn away from her."

Devereaux stared into the depths of Solowey's eyes, then dropped his gaze. "I walked out," he said.

"A misbegotten child, a loveless child," Solowey said. "Think of her story. She found her father, love, found the shining promise that would redeem the lost years. And think of how it was taken from her. Think of the way Frankie

184

Hughes was murdered, Devereaux! It was something to know, an agony for the living to endure." He shook his head. "Too much, Devereaux. Too great an agony for just a driven girl. Who could be as stoic as that? Who could hold to sanity?"

"I walked out," Devereaux said, closing his eyes.

I see her now in my mind's eye. I see her impaled on the iron railing spikes.

"You weren't just a finger man, Devereaux. You were much more to her, something much finer."

"It was murder," Devereaux said emptily. "It wasn't just that my pride was hurt. It was murder, and I'm a policeman. I'm a policeman, not a judge."

"Just a cop," he heard Solowey say.

"Just a tough cop," Solowey said again, shaking his head from side to side, as if all of his wisdom stood helpless before this one thing.

Just a tough cop. The words were separate weights that fell with a thud on Devereaux's heart.

THE END